Fishes is the debut work of detective writer Ricky Ren. The book, along with philosophical reasoning, partially reflects the moments of the author's biography. Being a Sinologist by the first education, Ricky Ren lived and worked for a long time in Guangzhou, Shanghai, and Hong Kong as an Ambassador for the French Cognac House. This unusual mix of cultures, traditions, and languages greatly weaved into a single incomparable adventure picture with the taste of rare French vintage.

To my beloved family, inspiring me to create,
To my best friend, inspiring me to grow,
To my first friend, who we miss so much.
Ricky Ren

Ricky Ren

FISHES

AUSTIN MACAULEY PUBLISHERS™
LONDON * CAMBRIDGE * NEW YORK * SHARJAH

Copyright © Ricky Ren 2023

All rights reserved. No part of this publication may be reproduced, distributed, or transmitted in any form or by any means, including photocopying, recording, or other electronic or mechanical methods, without the prior written permission of the publisher, except in the case of brief quotations embodied in critical reviews and certain other non-commercial uses permitted by copyright law. For permission requests, write to the publisher.

Any person who commits any unauthorized act in relation to this publication may be liable to criminal prosecution and civil claims for damages.

This is a work of fiction. Names, characters, businesses, places, events, locales, and incidents are either the products of the author's imagination or used in a fictitious manner. Any resemblance to actual persons, living or dead, or actual events is purely coincidental.

Ordering Information
Quantity sales: Special discounts are available on quantity purchases by corporations, associations, and others. For details, contact the publisher at the address below.

Publisher's Cataloging-in-Publication data
Ren, Ricky
Fishes

ISBN 9781685622398 (Paperback)
ISBN 9781685622404 (ePub e-book)

Library of Congress Control Number: 2022922698

www.austinmacauley.com/us

First Published 2023
Austin Macauley Publishers LLC
40 Wall Street,33rd Floor, Suite 3302
New York, NY 10005
USA

mail-usa@austinmacauley.com
+1 (646) 5125767

Many thanks for entire team of Austin Macauley Publishers, LLC for giving me an opportunity to publish this work.

Chapter 1
The Torch

Eight minutes to midnight according to Paris Time… Almost in the dark, Henri fastens his custom-made platinum cufflinks, glancing down at the formidable octopus-shaped ceramic clock watching him from the opposite wall. Carefully straightening his tie, covered in a thin layer of 24-carat gold, he nervously monitors the movement of the second hand. Six more minutes…

Looking down at the open bottle of Lero's family reserve cognac, he immediately remembered the half-empty glass of Jamaican coffee, carelessly left by him somewhere on the desk at the opposite end of the room. Along with the five cigars he had smoked on that long night, he carefully performed his grandfather's favorite tasting ritual. Coffee, Cognac, Cigar – exactly as old Jean taught them.

Five minutes to midnight… Pressing the button to automatically open the blinds, Henri struggles to his feet, slowly lights up a cigarette, and moves toward a huge panoramic window that opens up the best views of morning Hong Kong… He moves to the center of the room, still not taking his eyes off this charming, technogenic panorama. It's just three and a half minutes more before midnight, but the silence was broken by the phone call.

'Monsieur Lero, you are disturbed by…' a low female voice addressed him.

'Not now!' he let out sharply. 'I'm waiting for an extremely important call.'

Two and a half minutes to midnight… Monsieur Lero's heart seemed to be beating in time with the wall-mounted ceramic octopus. Two minutes to midnight…call.

'Already…' the young man quietly uttered at the opposite end of the line.

'Already? Jules, but it's only 11:58 in Paris…' Henri confusingly looked at the clock. 'How?' He dug his nails into the armrest of the chair.

'Just like grandfather... And Uncle Jacques...' Jules answered with a trembling voice. 'Will you come?'

'Of course. Not every night my younger brother dies,' Henri replied, hanging up.

It was still only one minute to midnight.

***

The road to Guangzhou Baiyun International Airport, named after Guangzhou's Baiyun Mountain, or "white cloud" mountain in Chinese, usually does not take more than an hour if you drive out from the business center of the city. Henri loved the road toward this mountain, which was one of his favorite places in the city.

Taking all the essentials from his small apartment along the famous Shangxiajiu Pedestrian Street, he leisurely went down the main elevator. According to his brief plan, he will first enjoy a little walk through the Beijing street, and visit the wholesale center of paintings and supplies for artists, where he will pick up a couple of pictures he has ordered to take home for Jules.

'Home...' slowly saying this word, Henri grumbled. It has been too long since he returned to Cognac or even Paris. It has been too long since he called that house his home.

Having walked in rather tight boots to the main intersection, he again scolded himself for once again forgetting to take an umbrella, which would be very useful in such hot sunshine, especially for such a Snow White as himself. After walking another three hundred meters to the art center, he realized that he was quite ready to change his cramped shoes to slates, despite the collapse of the perfect image, carefully calibrated by him in the morning. Linen suits often saved Henri when the choice stood between the option of dressing lightly or however he liked.

Elegant three-piece suits had become perhaps his main expense for quite some time, except perhaps the collectible figures from our thirty-three-year-old friend's favorite masterpieces of Japanese animation. Those that the eldest of his younger brothers, Thomas, had once rudely called dolls.

'Thomas...' Another drip of sweat ran down Henri's back, and he felt a chill.

Glancing casually at the watch worn on his left wrist, which sometimes trembled slightly from his youth, he noted that the minute hand was already running up to ten minutes past three. Once again mentally scolding himself for his slowness, he moved sharply to the main entrance of the wholesale art center.

After finishing with the paintings, he safely reached the airport and surprisingly, without any problems checking in his luggage, Henri took his place on board and was ready for fifteen minutes of drinking some "no name, no year, no sort" red wine from a plastic cup. At least unknown to him and the flight attendant. Considering the huge number of passengers flying on this charter flight, he did not want to be unkind toward the flight attendants, but curiosity tempted him to make sure that the harvest year was correctly determined by him.

Accidentally receiving hand luggage in the forehead from a lady of advanced age unknown to him, Henri noted with a grin that such a picture would greatly amuse his late father. A former heir to the cognac empire Lero gets drunk in a crowded economy class cabin.

Nice, Henri thought and asked for a refill his drink.

After five hours of travel, the main bonus on this flight was a tolerable window seat and a still half-charged e-book with a downloaded collection of Jules Verne's best novels. Glancing at his watch, Henri fixed his gaze on the second hand, slowly approaching midnight.

'Tick-tock... Tick-tock... Tick-tock...' whispered the wristwatch. 'Tick-tock... Tick-tock... Tick-tock...' Three heartbeats for each knock. 'Tick-tock... Tick-tock...' Two beats. 'T-ic...' The mechanical heart of the wristwatch begins to stop. Henri's left eye begins to twitch nervously, but he doesn't take his eyes off the clock hands, which are slowly covered with carved lines, fancifully increasing in size and bent by the tentacles of a small brown octopus. Henri involuntarily turned his gaze from the watch to his own hands, which at that moment were rapidly decreasing in size and losing their usual thick hairline. 'Tick... Tick...' Wristwatches suddenly stop. Henri watches as they slowly crawl from his wrist to the wall until a child's voice to his right interrupts this truly eerie sight.

"They've brought a new catfish," the red-haired boy with sky-blue eyes, and a drop of sweat over his upper lip, shouted enthusiastically.

The boy intermittently tugged on Henri by the sleeve of a red and black striped chunky knit jumper.

'Thomas...' Astonished, Henri puts his hand over his ten-year-old younger brother's hand, unable to hold back his tears. 'Alive...'

'Henri and Torch, what are you digging there?' grumbled a plump, blond kid who had flown into the room, shifting a small fishing net invitingly from one hand to another.

'Jules, why are you calling me Torch again? If you like being called Guppy, then be kind and pick another nickname for our older brother, otherwise, he will be the only one of us without a "Fish nickname."'

'Just Henri...' the redhead began with a stern frown.

'He cannot see his fish essence from this side, silly. You should look outside of something if you want to see it. How can he tell us what kind of fish he is from his inside?' Raising his eyebrows high, the curly-haired toddler answered, spinning a small pretzel on his finger that he had pulled out of his pants pocket.

'Then why are you calling me Torch? On what planet did you hear about a fish like that, Henri?' asked Thomas, perplexed, rolling his eyes capriciously.

'You don't look like a fish, Thomas,' he retorted without taking a look at his brother.

'Never did... The only one who didn't look like... There is no place for you underwater...' finished Henri, wiping away the tears with his sleeve.

'Why is he whining?' The youngest boy stared at him blankly. "Did he re-read, 'The Mysterious Island' again, or did he spat his poetry again to someone?" he asked, tapping on Thomas's leg.

'Jules, it's correct to say "spout poetry," not spit poetry.'

'Oh, yes Henri, if you can live without writing – please do not write,' he agreed with the younger boy, the middle one of Lero's sons, adding, 'maybe you also should forget about painting, because your pictures... They're too specific.'

'Yes, worse than mine. Here, look.' With a chubby palm, the four-year-old child takes a folded notebook from his left pocket. Jules is depicted in the center of the picture. On the right, the child was being hugged by the head of the family, Albert Lero, next to whom the kid placed his uncle Jacques. On the left, the artist had depicted Henri, who was being hugged by Thomas. In the upper right corner was a beautiful white angel who looked sadly down on the family members.

'This is Mom,' he said, pointing a finger at the angel, which was sadly confirmed by the baby. 'And these are your flock of girls.' He giggled viciously, pointing to a large number of black dots next to the face of the painted Henri.

Thomas held on to his sides, barely managing to stand, he was laughing so much. Little Jules giggled contentedly, landing on the edge of the striped carpet in the center of the large hall, and Henri, straightening his long black emo bangs, beloved by the fourteen-year-old him, and a flock of those girls, examined the drawing in his hands. He remembered that evening. It was their last evening together when no one could have suspected that in just twenty-eight hours their lives would change irrevocably.

'Henri!' Thomas shouted suddenly. 'Fasten!'

Henri turned his head and was already intending to say something, as he felt the touch of someone else's palm on his left shoulder.

'Sir, please fasten your seat belt. Our plane is beginning its descent.' Smilingly smiling...the flight attendant addresses him.

Not fully awake from such a realistic dream, Henri silently nodded and followed her instructions.

The rest of the journey was fairly calm. Having successfully passed through the security checks after landing, he, anticipating the upcoming hours of journey on the road from Paris to his hometown of Cognac, decided to have a bite of his favorite quiche Lorraine with salmon in a café on the first floor of the airport. Having dealt with breakfast rather quickly, Henri, slowly sipping a latte, went to the agreed meeting point to wait for the driver. The car he had ordered wasn't long in coming, and after four hours of travel, they finally arrived at their destination.

The evenings were warm here at this time of the year, fortunately, a pattern that for the many years of his absence, never left this paradise. Small semi-sprawled houses, somewhere chic, large estates and, of course, hectares of white grapes.

'Haven't seen you for a long time,' Monsieur Ugni blanc, whispered to him, as he greedily inhaled the aroma of one of the main sorts of grape for the production of cognac through the open window. Old Jean's lessons about the secrets of a true cellar master came back to mind. Here, timely harvesting, correct spinning, fermentation that meets all the requirements, a double distillation of jewelry work, and, of course, exemplary aging in special barrels from Tronsoy oak are important.

'CHTTHZZ.' Another steep bump interrupted the flow of Henri's thoughts.

'Sorry,' the rosy-cheeked driver said, smiling. 'Roads here are not the best.'

'Yes,' Henri agreed bitterly. 'Where do our taxes go?' he added, raising his eyebrows.

'Exactly! From one year to the next, there are so many complaints, so much noise, but nothing changes. Neither the road nor the working conditions,' the driver indignantly echoed twirling his mustache.

'It's surprising that all this is happening after the landing on the Moon,' said Henri, perplexed raising his hands.

'We're just like the stones on this road,' the driver drawled thoughtfully, turning off the main highway. 'They threw it in a heap, called it France, and forgot it.'

'Yes, and note, stones of Earth origin. If we were from the Moon, we would instantly gain value. We would be lying peacefully in the planetarium under the glass.' Henri noted, looking thoughtfully out of the window.

'It's good that the ravine has been fenced off,' the driver began anxiously. 'This road in the rain is like butter. So many people have disappeared, for example...' He already intended to tell his story but was immediately interrupted by Henri.

'Here to the right,' his passenger blurted out sharply, nervously rubbing his palms. 'Please stop at Lero's manor.'

'As you wish,' the driver replied, looking blankly at Henri over his shoulder.

Henri pressed himself tightly into the back seat and closed his eyes in an attempt to calm down a little. *Eight... Seven... Six... Five... Four... Three... Two... One... Breathe out.*

'Well, here we are,' the driver announced happily, parking in front of the destination.

The gates of the house have not changed a bit since the last time Henri left it behind, sitting inside his father's Bugatti Royale.

'Beautiful house. Have you arrived for the party?' the driver asked Henri as he helped him to get the paintings out of the trunk.

'Yes, to the funeral,' Henri answered him, catching the bewildered look of his interlocutor. 'In our family, it is mandatory to celebrate each funeral, so this is a kind of party. Will you join me for tea?'

'Oh,' the driver began, confused, 'thanks, but I still have a couple of places to go, so I have to rush off. Have a nice day!'

'Thank you, too. I was glad to meet you!' answered Henri, shaking his hand.

Turning to the house, he glanced at his watch and was surprised to find that the time was already approaching two. With all the preparations for the funeral, he had only four hours to sort things out and put himself in order. Taking a deep breath, Henri grabbed the weighty suitcase, suddenly feeling that his left arm was getting a little heavier than usual.

Well, right, he thought, *the closer to the Torch, the harder.*

The opening gates were immediately filled with several unknown men. Henri thought that they probably should be the head of the guard, the butler, and someone from the Lero Cognac House.

'Good afternoon, Monsieur Lero,' said a gray-haired man, who looked about sixty years old. 'Let me introduce myself. My name is François de Galhau. I have been the butler of this house for the last fifteen years, and this is Jean-Yves Parly, head of security.' Jean-Yves nodded respectfully. 'Let me also introduce our good friend Jacques Guillaume. He is the Cognac cellar master.'

'Nice to meet you, gentlemen.' Henri shook hands with his interlocutors with the best of his smiles and even added about three percent of his charm to this as a sign of special gratitude. In this conversation with the people on whose shoulders this huge house had been held in recent years, he felt like the prodigal son.

'It's a great honor to finally meet you, Monsieur Lero. We heard so much about you from your brother,' added Jacques smiling.

'Just Henri.' He smiled in response and apologizing for the suddenness of his appearance, as he slowly walked to the house. He was embarrassed to take everyone away from their affairs.

After passing about a hundred meters through a small alley, Henri finally came close to the house. The same white brick, but the roof now having been diligently painted blue, hiding any mention that, historically, it had been a bright red hue. An old metal vane with a cockerel still decorated the roof, not changing at all over the years. In general, the building can look rather sleazy, if there is no badly rusted cornice, which revives the memory of the feeling of redness, which could not be scratched from his memories even now.

Unlocking the main door, Henri walked into a spacious living room filled with bright dining light. From the portrait on the opposite wall, all the smiling members of the Lero family looked down at him.

In the center of the painting towered the majestic father of the family in a strict, dark-red three-piece suit, complemented by a classic black butterfly. He held the shoulders of his senior heirs: eight-year-old Thomas, dressed in a dark blue satin suit and an elegant black shirt with a steel-colored tie, and twelve-year-old Henri with neatly laid, slightly long dark hair. He was wearing a dark green three-piece suit in black stripes, the same style black shirt as Thomas was wearing, and a dark green tie. To his father's right stood their uncle Jacques in a dark cherry suit with a vest. In the center of the picture sat the beautiful blond mother of the boys – Madame Maria Lero, in a sky-blue dress and burgundy boater-shoes. In her arms, she carefully held the fair-haired baby, Jules, dressed in a dark brown suit, and tightly clutching in his hands the figure of a chess elephant.

'Tick-tock... Tick-tock...' Henri with sadness took his eyes off the picture and looked at the clock. It was five minutes to three. He caught a glimpse of the staircase, where, according to Jules, his children's room still awaited him.

Having easily crossed two floors, Henri habitually popped to the end of the corridor, as if he had not been away these last nineteen years.

Body memory is a great thing. Henri often regretted that this phenomenon did not apply to other areas. For many years of his life with his Aunt Selena in Hong Kong, and then after moving to Guangzhou a few years ago, he was never able to learn Chinese. Not that this was the first thing Henri could not count among his victories, but at the proper level he spoke in Latin, and even understand a little bit in Japanese and Korean, but Chinese... Henri grumbled. Learning Chinese in many ways reminded him of a leap of faith: you have been praying hard for several years, praying and waiting for a miracle, which, as his interpreter friends said, comes not to everyone and only after two or three years of study. Whether he prayed badly, whether faith in his heart was not enough or whether the stumbling block was the main root of evil – a knowledge of English.

'Knowledge of English always corrupts when you can get whatever you want only by using English.' He noted, finally reaching the end of the corridor and opening the door to his room.

Pushing back against the door, Henri dragged the suitcase inside, surprised to find that his chest of drawers had moved from the left to the right side, closer to the window. He found his glazed collection of anime figures in the former place – along the left wall of the room, but arranged in a completely different order. The figures were sorted thematically and stood exactly in a row at a perfectly measured distance from each other – about two centimeters from the wall and a half centimeter between each other.

Finally, you got to my dolls, Mr. Red-Hair Perfectionist, Henri noted with a smile, leaving the paintings on the floor near the right wall.

After slowly coming closer to the rack with the collection, he sat down on a chair opposite to it, looking around with an admiring glance at all this strict splendor. Reviewing the figures, he imagined Thomas, moving them one by one, mentally scolding Henri for the eternal chaos in his life and his room, for his apathy and unwillingness to take responsibility, for his cowardice and for that night…the night when he almost killed little Jules…

Henri squeezed his trembling left hand painfully, trying to soothe the tears flowing down his face, until he stopped his gaze on a figure in armor depicting the character of Alphonse Elric, from the anime, *"Fullmetal Alchemist,"* that for some reason, left the ranks of the thematically close neighbors on the shelf. The figurine stood alone on the floor, exactly two centimeters from the rack. Leaning over, taking it in his hands, and smiling sadly, he put it away in the right pocket of his jacket.

After taking a shower and sorting things out, Henri noted that there was about an hour before the funeral, and decided to sit for a while on the balcony, where he often managed to smoke in secret from his parents. The balcony successfully opened onto the vineyard, so that it was impossible to see him from the central gate or the neighboring houses. Sitting comfortably in an old rattan chair, he leisurely took a couple of puffs of French Gitanes cigarettes, carefully hidden by him in a small gap between the seventh and eighth bricks of the third row from the left-hand side of the entrance to the balcony. He remembers that he once made this cache together with someone from his "flock of girls."

With whom did I hide these cigarettes? Henri thought for a second, looking somewhere into the distance, and suddenly turned pale. 'Marie-Julie...'

The cigarette immediately fell out of his hand, painfully burning his leg and leaving traces of ash on his perfectly white bathrobe. Memories suddenly flashed out... Her always detached doll's gray eyes, lively chestnut curls, bronze skin, and of course, a strange expression of sadness and boredom that never left this girl's face. Henri turned around, hearing a rustle behind him... But there was no one there.

think I she asked me about something in our last meeting... I think it was in her room, – Henri reasoned, looking nervously beyond the horizon, where the top of the still crimson canopy of the Langlais family estate was barely visible.

Henri tried desperately to remember what she asked him then, but no matter how hard he tried, he could not come close to the answer. He only remembered how they smoked, lounging right there on her bed. She purred something slowly about life in general, complained about her twin brother, Charles, and his constant clashes with their father. Charles was generally a strange guy, literally obsessed with the correct order of things. Sometimes, Henri thought that all Charles's actions boiled down to tracking imperfections around. Interestingly, that Henri himself was at a top of the list with these imperfections, since, according to Charles, the "nasty emo boy" had a very bad influence on his sister.

Oh, it would be funny if he found us smoking right in her room, he thought smiling. 'Although Charles, despite his slenderness, was still older either by two or by three years, which is why he was almost two heads taller. So if he had caught me then, he would probably have thoroughly beaten me,' Henri concluded. 'Marie-Julie, by the way... She was also tall... She was...'

Henri's thread of memory was cut off with a sharp bang just above his left ear.

'I left you in the house alone for only a few hours, and you've already turned it into a pigsty.' A tall, fair-haired young man appeared on the balcony, smiling and pointing to the smoking cigarette butt that had accidentally dropped from Henri's hands.

'My dear brother Jules, why, despite the fact I heroically saved this white bathrobe from injury with my beautiful leg, are you wafting dirty insinuations in my direction,' Henri said innocently, pointing to a small burn where the cigarette had dropped on his left ankle.

'You mean, your hairy leg of Australopithecus?' That did not appease the younger of the brothers, defiantly showing his almost hairless leg, covered only with a light white down.

'You have your whole life ahead of you. When you reach my age, your hair will grow out of your ears…sprouting in all directions,' Henri continued, raising his eyebrows slightly. 'Right over your whole face, so you will have to shave them off like this.' He colorfully demonstrated the process with his right hand. 'From ear to ear horizontally, there to your Adam's apple, and then up to the eyes for the second time, but vertically.' He calmly held out his hand and forcefully pinched his younger brother.

'Okay, that's enough. Don't hurt your little brother.' Laughed Jules as he attempted to wriggle out of the next tweak.

'First, you are already twenty-three years old, and this is the average life expectancy in ancient Egypt. And secondly, my little one, you have already grown to such a size that you are one and a half heads taller than me,' Henri said as he continued the furious attacks on his brother.

'No, no… Break.' Grabbing his older brother by the shoulders, Jules began diligently suppressing another fit of laughter. 'It's time for us to go down to the ceremony.'

'Okay, I'll join you in five minutes,' Henri replied, nodding toward the suit he had laid out in readiness on the bed.

Jules nodded silently and, patting his brother on the shoulder, quickly left the room.

Going downstairs, Henri found that the reception hall was already full of guests who, according to their butler Francois, began arriving about five-thirty. According to the old tradition of the Lero family, guests were always greeted with cocktails made with a two-year-old Lero Cognac House's VS. As a rule, at all the events at the House, the bartender must mix such famous cognac cocktails as "Sidecar" and "French Connection," as well as Lero's branded drinks of their own recipe, among which were "Empire Lero," first mixed in the year 1945, by their ancestor and the founder of the Cognac House – Carl-Louis Lero, and the cocktail "Fall of Zion," which, ironically, was created by the main star of this show, the deceased Thomas Lero.

Another good tradition of the family was that regardless of the type of event, it was customary that music which was preferred by the owner of the evening should be played during the activity. In keeping with this tradition, light melodic jazz was being played in the house, which made the funeral look like some romantic date.

'You were perfect even in this, Torch,' Henri whispered, drinking "The Fall of Zion" and walking into the center of the hall through a noisy crowd of guests, to view his deceased brother, lying peacefully in in his coffin. 'Perfect evening; as perfect as you. Well, maybe except for the cufflinks. They picked some terrible cufflinks for you.'

'Do you think that the Torch would organize everything ten times better if the situation was reversed and it was your funeral, or mine?' Jules asked as he took a drink from his glass of "Fall of Zion." 'I mean, if it were me, techno would be thumping a beat through the house, and in your case, even worse – we would make a three-hour audio recording of your sad, suicidal poems and all the walls would be decorated with your asymmetric daub.'

'You shouldn't be talking about daub. I just brought a couple of my latest works with me, so you will be pleasantly surprised, brother. I grew up as an artist.'

'Come on.' Raising his right eyebrow skeptically, Jules sneered.

'Of course, you haven't seen my works for nineteen years,' the older brother continued.

'I've come to see you every summer during the last eight years, but I couldn't find a single correct diagonal in your nest,' Jules remarked, greedily gulping down the remnants of the cocktail. 'Well, what will you say?'

'One word, Jules: techno!' Henri stretched out with disgust. 'Seven years in music school… What a shame!'

'That's true,' Jules agreed guiltily.

The brothers silently looked at the open coffin of their deceased brother, each thinking about his own. The waiters entered the hall with glasses of Lero's four years old VSOP cognac, which marked the beginning of the funeral service. The guests immediately began to sit down along the rows of chairs set out ready, and Henri noted that about fifty people were present in the main hall now. After looking around for a bit, he decided to sit at the end of the room, choosing a large leather chair as his location, directly under a painting depicting a scene in which three robots were disembarking from their spacecraft, onto the surface of Jupiter.

The Holy Father began the service and asked the youngest of the brothers to say a few words about the deceased.

'Thomas liked to say that when he leaves this world, there will be two things he will regret: the first one, if Tyrion Lannister does not take the iron throne in the final book of the well-known saga.' The guests laughed together, and after waiting for a short pause, he continued, 'If you don't know who that is, then just leave this room.' The audience burst into laughter again, and a couple of Thomas's close friends even applauded. 'And the second one, if his older brother Henri will not read one of his wonderful poems at his funeral.' Jules with a sly smile looked at his brother, who was sitting at the opposite end of the room, so everyone present immediately turned toward him.

'Red pest,' Henri whispered, smiling. 'You catch me even after death, Thomas.'

Henri got up grandly from his chair and walked slowly into the center of the room.

'He asked me to tell you that the score is 1:0,' patting him on the shoulder, Jules whispered, leaving Henri alone to stand in front of the gathered guests.

Henri was a little confused, diligently looking at the guests who had come. Among them were different faces: pale and swarthy, elongated and wide, European, Negroid and even a couple of Asian guests; there were many brown-eyed and a lot of blue-eyed, Greek and cursed noses; here sat thin-lipped and plump guests, bearded and freckled. They, perhaps, had nothing in common at first glance, but one thing still gave out in them a common feature of all Thomas's friends – a bright, incomparably sincere smile. The smile with which Thomas himself always smiled.

Henri translated the view from the guests to his dead brother, peaceably lying to his right. He saw Thomas so close for the first time in the last nineteen years. Bright red hair still sparkled in the soft light of the floor lamps. The perfectly straight nose continued straight, brownish eyebrows, lips relaxed, but even now there was a sense that they are about to blur in a contented smile.

> At the heaven's edge birds are pinching,
> Tearing clouds apart, like flocks.
> Gray yarn near us is still spreading,

But the spindle burns like a torch.
People with the world are still spinning and spinning
And I've been dreaming for so many days and nights.
How the sea above us will finally shrivel,
And the sun will crash down to the empty ground.

Having finished his verse, Henri carefully examined the faces of the assembled guests and noticed that most of them looked a little puzzled.

'If anyone is interested, please leave your request for the purchasing of a three-hour audio version of this masterpiece,' he said with a smile, causing a wave of amicable laughter.

'It's time to start preparations for my funeral,' Henri whispered, standing next to a slyly smiling Jules, who at that moment had just turned off the voice recorder.

The funeral service ended around six-thirty and most of the guests left the house at about nine pm. Jules and Henri spent about half an hour in the kitchen and the main hall, helping the service staff to finish cleaning as soon as possible, so they could begin the informal commemoration of Lero's circle early.

Throughout this informal ceremony, close relatives told each other different stories about the deceased and talked about things that they wanted, or could have together. The traditional part of the commemoration was the tasting of ten-year-old Lero XO cognac and at midnight, when the eldest of the family said the last words, the relatives drank a glass of 20-year-old Lero Extra and bid farewell to the deceased forever. From the outside, the whole process seemed reminiscent of a long evening of Cognac tasting with elements of the dark Gothic.

Henri untied his tight-fitting tie and looked defiantly at the same bronze octopus watch, a copy of which he had placed in his Hong Kong office. After making sure that the hands of the clock showed exactly ten, Henri did not wait for a special invitation but opened a corked bottle of Lero XO. Jules at this time took off his shoes, sitting comfortably in a chair by the fireplace with his feet resting on a soft ottoman. His hair, so perfectly groomed two hours ago, but now slightly disheveled, Jules reached for a glass. Sitting next to him, Henri got the ceremony started by opening the conversation.

'Jules... That was his name,' Henri whispered, mysteriously looking into the fire.

'Sorry, what?' Choking and continuing to cough in laughter, the younger of the two brothers was perplexed.

'Our lizard. Henri explained with a smile. 'When Thomas was five, Dad, Mom, and Uncle took us on our first real fishing trip. The Torch was so excited that he couldn't sleep for two nights before the upcoming trip.' Henri smiled slightly at Jules, noticing his keen interest in this story. 'We were very well prepared, taking with us three books about the definition of different types of fish, four nets, three types of fishing line, two rods, and even for some reason, we dragged fish food from our mother's aquarium and some three-liter jars for the fish we would catch.'

Henri drank a little from the glass, noting that the cognac of this crop was simply amazingly good.

'The road to the river took more than three hours, and if you take into account the lack of sleep for the previous two nights, and the weak vestibular apparatus of our middle brother, it is easy to understand that his state of health on his birthday was terrible. But despite any persuasion, our stubborn hero did not succumb to common pleas, and instead of peacefully dreaming in the cozy interior of our father's Bugatti, he stoically fished on the shore in his little blue rubber boots.' Henri continued, causing Jules to smile again, 'So, by the second hour, when he realized that fishing was not going well, a dull and very sleepy Thomas decided to get a couple of fatty earthworms from somewhere. We had been wandering along the rocky shore for about twenty minutes when we decided to dig a hole-trap for the earthworms. We put a jar of fish food in the hole, which should, of course, have attracted all the worms in the area. We laid a trap and began to wait. We waited for about half an hour until we both fell into a dead sleep. I distinctly remember that then I dreamed about Aneta, a blonde girl with a beautiful bob hairstyle, who gave me a plasticine beetle in the last year of kindergarten.'

'I've always been a ladies' man,' he drawled cheerfully, inhaling the unique notes of a leather purse and sandalwood from his glass.

'So, I quietly slept, seeing in my dream a blond angel with a plasticine beetle, until someone's loud cry pulled me out of the kingdom of Morpheus. When I woke up, I saw in front of me the roaring Thomas, furiously rubbing his eyes and tightly holding that jar with fish food.'

'Henri,' he said to me. 'Henri...' I could not even imagine... I was so tired, I felt so bad, and I didn't expect anything. I didn't even hope for a small fish or a fly, and there he was… He handed me that jar at the bottom of which lay a small lizard, peacefully curled up in a ball. Let's call him Jules, he said smiling, and he couldn't stop smiling through his tears. I've never seen him so happy,' Henri continued.

'Jules lived with us for about a year, until one day the Torch and I couldn't find him. He just disappeared. Thomas didn't leave the room for a week, ate poorly, and hardly talked to anyone. Until one evening just before his sixth birthday, when mother gathered us all in the living room and said that Thomas and I would soon have a younger brother.' Henri looked at Jules's dumbfounded eyes, setting his glass aside. 'Thomas then burst into tears, ran up to Mom, and, hugging her big belly, said that we should call you Jules. And that's what we called you.' After finishing the story, Henri drained his glass and carefully put it on a small marble table by the fireplace.

'Unbelievable…' Jules whispered without blinking, gazing into the fire. 'In honor of the lizard…'

'Jules wasn't an ordinary lizard,' Henri said, smiling with the corner of his mouth. "I suppose he would be proud of his namesake if he could meet you like that. How proud Thomas was, always was." Henri put his left hand on Jules's shoulder and patted him lightly.

'It's still trembling a little,' Jules remarked, not taking his eyes off from his brother's left hand. 'How did it happen then? We never really talked about it.' The younger brother looked at Henri sympathetically.

'I…' Henri started but decided to first top up the XO in their glasses. 'On that evening, Uncle Jacques and I were sitting in the guest room near mother's aquarium, surrounded by several fish encyclopedias. It was that evening that a few new catfish were bought, so uncle undertook to help me with our fish register.' Jules nodded approvingly because he remembered well how carefully they treated and loved this mother's hobby…

The brothers regularly entered all the inhabitants of "Eridu" into their register, conscientiously conducting a census of its citizens. Such an approach helped them to calculate the necessary amount of food, confirm the best time for aquarium cleaning, and get a better understanding of whether all the fish live peacefully with each other.

'We were almost done when uncle left for initiation…' Henri paused, and Jules began nervously spinning a glass in his hand. 'I didn't believe in all this "curse" at that time, but I still vaguely remembered what happened to our grandfather when he tried to head the Trust instead of the acting Guardian from the Kebe family. I was only six when it happened to grandfather... I often thought that all this could be just a dream. He was already over eighty then... Anything could happen and anything could have been seen. At least our father convinced me of this. At fourteen, I considered myself old enough to agree with father's arguments, but...I was afraid, Jules, I was very afraid for our uncle. I wasn't allowed to enter the common hall, so I spent most of the time sitting opposite the entrance in front of the door. I remember the sound of applause, which marked the beginning of the meeting, then the audience quieted down, and someone took the floor. What it was about, I couldn't make out, but I was reassured by the fact that I didn't hear any screams. This went on for about fifteen minutes, during which I desperately awaited repeated applause, which would mean that the official order had nevertheless been signed. According to the stories of the curse that have come down to us, the signing is the most important sign that Zindae has accepted the applicant as heir.'

'Zindae Kebe, the foundation's first Keeper?' Jules clarified certainly.

'Yes, the one who first saved the property of the founding families during the war, for which he was appointed in 1945 as Custodian of all funds of the Trust. The first and main manager of the Trust. The one who cursed all its members for trying to do business behind his back.

'The charter of the Trust still stipulates that only the Kebe's family Guardian can be the manager of the funds.'

'And to be more precise,' explained Henri, looking at the fire in the fireplace through the glass, the male heir of Kebe family. This became a loophole for the founding families, because, in the absence of a male heir from Kebe's side, one of the heads of the founding families can formally serve as a temporary Guardian.'

'And of all the heads of the founding families who tried to head the foundation... Since then...no one came to sign the order during initiation?'

'If I were to believe what I've heard, then no. A couple of people had time to put part of their signatures, like our grandfather. It formally made the head of the Trust his widow, our grandmother, as temporary guardian.

'By the way, nobody told us about grandmother's death until uncle's initiation,' Jules whispered bitterly.

'As I understand it, they kept it under wraps, fearing that other founding houses might want to introduce their candidates for initiation. For this reason, the announcement was made right at the annual meeting, the day before uncle's initiation. Since uncle Jacques did not have a wife, he could appoint our father as the Guardian regent in case of his death.'

'So signing is the final part of the curse? I mean, everything would be okay if you pass it on?'

'I wanted to believe it then. The last time, when I was sitting in the same chair, waiting for grandfather… Instead of hearing repeated applause, I just heard screams of horror that made me rush into the hall and see what I saw then. And now, after only eight years, I waited again… I waited until the time again approached midnight, like the last time, as in those same stories about the curse of the Trust. The clock showed thirty seconds to midnight when I heard a deafening sound of applause. Then I thought that this was the happiest moment in my life. I stopped being happy about anything since our mother passed away, but that applause seemed to wrest me out of the darkness. Not remembering myself with joy, I burst into the hall when the clock with the bronze octopus showed five seconds to midnight. At first, uncle was very scared when he saw me at the door, but then he also turned his gaze to the clock… We laughed together… He almost could… Almost… The second hand was at three seconds before midnight, when…from his eyes…' Henri looked down. 'Blood… Blood began… Blood began to flow from his eyes, then he grabbed his heart and fell on the table. Unfortunately, his torment did not end there. Uncle was convulsing for two more seconds until he raised his head and looked at me for the last time, after which he collapsed on the table and never got up again… Never… The clock, like then with his grandfather, was exactly midnight.' Henri silently looked into the glass for a while, unable to continue the story. 'I, then…' the elder began again, 'seeing all of this then… I remembered everything. I saw the same thing with our grandfather… Blood from his eyes, convulsions, and exactly at midnight on the clock… And our father… Father saw it too… He stood just two steps to grandpa's right that night. He saw it for sure… He knew everything… He knew and let our uncle… For the money… For the damn money…' Henri buried his hands in his hair and slowly exhaled. 'I hardly remember how I came to the nursery… I only remember how I told Thomas something about uncle and father, something about our escape, that we have to leave this place altogether so that father would not send us all to be slaughtered. Just like he did with uncle. I talked and talked, but he didn't listen to me at all. I grabbed his arms and tried to drag him with me, but despite the four-year difference, Thomas was a tough guy, and all my attempts seemed insignificant. And then I… I pushed him…'

Henri took a look at the late Thomas, with some force squeezing the armrest of the chair.

'Before realizing how wrong I was to try to force him out of the house, I got a few sweeps from Thomas, after which we finally began a productive conversation. He convinced me that together we would find out everything from father and uncle. He believed that everything would be okay. Going downstairs, we found that the first floor was full of people who were rushing about the house in a panic, and our father was standing in the middle of all this chaos. Thomas was the first to go up to him and say something in his ear, after which two of father's henchmen tied me up and dragged me by force into the guest room. Father and Thomas walked silently behind me until father quickened his pace and entered the guest room without closing the door. He gave me such a slap in the face, which he was only capable of doing without switching to a blow. "How dare you?" he shouted at me then. "How dare you smoke this stuff in my house? Again!" as he said this, he pressed his palm into my face one more time. "How could you also drag your little brother into it?" I looked into the corridor and saw Thomas standing there with a look of condemnation on his face… He did not believe me… Not a single word I'd said. Most likely, then in the hallway, he whispered to father that I was smoking marijuana again. He didn't believe me… He decided that…I would again… But that was the only time, right after mam was gone… That loss was too hard to stand it with a sober mind.'

Henri didn't take his eyes off the wall clock with the bronze octopus, and Jules silently stared at the floor.

'Father knew everything and saw everything, but I still couldn't understand why he needed all of this circus. I shouted to Thomas that dad was lying and that he always knew what would happen to uncle. Right after that father hit me again, but for real this time. Thomas stood silently in the corridor for a while, but then he went up to our father, hugged him, and said that they should go to uncle. The rest of it I remember only very vaguely… I only remember how I tried to grab Thomas, drag him away from our father by force. I remember how he kicked me and our father desperately tried to pull us apart. I remember how

I pushed them both sharply aside, and how Thomas flew into Mom's aquarium... Our beautiful "Eridu" crumbled into hundreds of pieces of glass... All our "fish citizens" flew to opposite sides of the room. Thomas, covered by bloody scratches, looked at me. He wasn't angry at all. He just shook his head anxiously, and whispered something.'

Henri looked at his brother.

'You know... I often wondered what happened to those fish? For some reason, it seemed to me that if they were not spoiled by our verified domestication, it would have been much easier for them. I still believe that they could very successfully coexist with each other in their natural environment, without calculations and restrictions, without this unnecessary glass box. We were buying their freedom for the illusion of security, but just for a moment – and then they were all scattered on the floor because of a fight between two boys. We never asked them if they wanted all this.'

Henri poured himself another XO and looked questioningly at his brother. Jules nodded slightly, not taking his sympathetic eyes off his older brother.

'I hardly remember how I grabbed one of the fish from the floor and ran out of the room. I found you in the nursery and put you in father's Bugatti. We quickly drove away from the house in the direction of the nearest gas station. On the way to which...I think that I stopped somewhere, but... I don't remember details... According to the plan, from the gas station, I would call our aunt Selena. I wanted to ask her to take us to her place in Hong Kong. We almost reached the bridge, but it started to rain so heavily that the street was turning into a wet ice rink, and then when we reached the ravine at the turn... I lost control, we turned over... When I woke up, father and Thomas were taking you by ambulance to the intensive care unit. I followed them to come with you. I remember how I put my hand on your shoulder... You could hardly breathe...' Henri exhaled heavily.

'Father then forcefully tore me away from you, saying that I shouldn't dare to touch you again. When the ambulance drove away, I saw Thomas keeping his distance. There was a heavy downpour; it was so wet and dark all around, but his eyes glowed like two torches. I tried to explain everything to him, but he wouldn't listen to me. We fought each other as best we could, until we simply rolled into a ravine, continuing to toss and turn in the mud.' Henri quickly drained his glass, placing it back on the marble table.

'Thomas hit me a few more times before getting to his feet. Turning his back to me, he said that he never wanted to see me again and after that, he walked quickly toward the road. I lay there, covered in mud for another ten minutes. Finally trying to get up, I realized that my left arm, on which Thomas landed when we fell into the ravine, was broken in several places. I walked to the gas station, called our aunt, and fell asleep right at the telephone booth. The next evening, I woke up at the house of her friends and two days later, she took me to Hong Kong. Our father didn't mind,' concluded Henri, leaning back in his chair and crossing his arms over his chest, exhaling deeply.

Jules silently nodded his head, looking from Henri to Thomas, resting in the coffin.

'He slept very badly for the last three months. I knew that he was hiding something from me and had been planning something for the last two years, but I could not figure out what. You know… We checked everything. Food, drinks, clothes, pen, paper. If one of the families kept poisoning us one by one, then at least some traces should have remained.' Jules unbuttoned the top buttons of his shirt and, following Henri's example, leaned back in his chair.

'Officially, the cause is still cardiac arrest,' began Henri. 'There are several dozens of poisons in the world that can cause a similar effect and leave no trace at the same time. But the question is who needs it all, and how they manage to do it over and over again, without attracting unnecessary attention. By the way, none of the representatives of the founding families were at the funeral. Neither the normally punctual Langlais, nor the Loup family who usually set an example to others, and no one from the Oak or Cigogne Houses. You wouldn't expect anything else from the Dragon couple; they're generally not very sociable anyway, but what about the Cartier and Aigle representatives? By the way, don't you find it odd that the Bernards didn't show up either? After all, for them, it would be such a convenient case to wipe the nose of the Aigles.

'I'd actually find it very frightening if they appeared,' Jules replied, rubbing his wrist. 'Their house burned down three months ago… The Bernard couple with their son. I'm sorry Henri, I remember that Oberon was your classmate.'

'Oberon…' Henri whispered, exhaling heavily. 'First, the Bernard family, then the heir of Lero House. It all looks like a story from a classic detective novel.'

'Yes, only with a voodoo element,' added Jules. 'You don't believe in this option at all?'

Henri looked at his watch and saw that it showed one minute to midnight. Taking a deep breath, he uncorked a new 20-year-old bottle of Lero Extra and carefully poured the cognac into the previously prepared tulip glasses with the high stem and narrow neck. 'Faith is the lot of young people, and I am only capable of skepticism and self-destruction,' he said fervently, stretching out a glass to his brother. 'For the Torch, who could have changed so much, but by the fact that he did not do it, he already changed a lot.'

'For the Torch,' Jules agreed and looking toward the coffin, added. 'I was thinking…Those cufflinks…'

Henri nodded silently and took off his own silver cufflinks in the shape of small ships. Carefully approaching the coffin, as if he was afraid to wake Thomas, he gently replaced the brass cufflinks in the form of anchors picked up by the organizers that Thomas was wearing. Silently joining him, Jules carefully removed the strands from the face of his deceased brother and kissed his forehead for the last time. After briefly standing at the coffin in silence, he nodded to Henri and silently left the room.

The clock was already half-past twelve, but Henri was still sitting in a leather armchair and looking at Thomas, peacefully lying in his coffin. He looked at him mournfully, gripping tightly in his hand the small figure he had found in his room that morning.

Chapter 2
Medusa

Tick-tock... Tick-tock... Tick-tock... The unfortunate clock with a bronze octopus still made Henri feel a trembling in his body, over and over again scrolling in his head scenes from the death of his grandfather and uncle.

'It's 2 am,' he stated with surprise, waking up in the same chair in the main hall, directly opposite the coffin of his late brother. Even though the chair was surprisingly comfortable, Henri reluctantly got up, intending to go to his bedroom. Shuffling loudly, he trudged along the long dark corridor, taking with him an opened bottle of Lero Extra.

'Ta-da-da... tra-da-da-da... da-da-ta... I don't remember how to sing it.' He whistled a half-forgotten rock ballad.

Ascending to the second floor, Henri hesitated a little, but as he approached his room, he began to hum, 'My scary beast, he is alone inside this dark... Get in and find a skeleton inside my thoughts... Here in my hand a TV remote, join with me!'

Let's fill our heads with trash and zeros. One, two, three!' Removing his left boot, Henri lost his balance for a second and almost dropped the twenty-year-old bottle of cognac on the floor. 'Stop... Crawl... Go... Run...Stop, crawl, go, run... Stop! Crawl! Go! Run! Stop, I warn you because I'm...'

'Behind you...' He heard the final remark of the chorus come from behind him, from the open door of the darkened room and, out of surprise, dropped the bottle.

Breathing heavily, Henri tried not to move. He was desperately trying to ignore what he'd heard. He was well aware that this strange guttural voice certainly did not belong to Jules or any of the staff. Even better, he understood that he did not want to see this, or the one to whom this voice belonged.

'I'm behind you,' the voice persisted from behind his back, but Henri still did not move.

'Behind! Behind! Behind! Behind! Behind!'

Unable to withstand such a disgusting screech, Henri clutched at his ears in pain and turned toward the sound. The voice died down instantly. The entire floor of the room was covered with crimson blood, in which a small aquarium fish slowly flopped about.

'Please, not on the bed,' he pleaded in a whisper, looking to the center of the room. 'Not on the bed... Not... She...'

But it was her. From the large wooden bed in the center of the room, two gray eyes were now glaring at him. The girl's head was twisted in an unnatural position. A shock of her long brown curls hung down like the tentacles of a jellyfish. The deathly pale hands were spread out on the bed as if the tendons had been cut on them, making their owner no longer able to control them. Her blood continued to flow from the thin veins onto the floor.

'You're late... Do you see that you're late?' the girl growled.

'Marie-Julie,' he began, lowering his eyes, but was immediately interrupted.

'Stop... Crawl... Go... Run...' she began.

'I...' He tried again.

'Stop, crawl, go, run... Stop! Crawl! Go! Run!'

'Listen!' he shouted.

'Run! Run! Run! Run! Run! Run! Run! Run! Run! Run! Run! Run! Run! Run! Run! Run! Run! Run! Run! Run! Run! Run! Run! Run! Run! Run! Run! Run! Run! Run!'

A terrible screech cut his ears so badly that he fell to the floor...

Cold sweat trickled down from Henri's forehead in large drops. Opening his eyes, he found himself still sitting in a leather armchair opposite a bronze clock with an octopus. It was 2 am... With a heavy sigh, Henri slowly walked to his room, looking back at the bottle of open "Lero Extra." After a little hesitation, he decided to leave the bottle downstairs. Henri quickly flew up the stairs to the bedroom, but slowed down a little as he approached the end of the hallway. The door was open again... Carefully, as if on ice, he made the last eight steps to the open door. Eight... Seven... Six... Five... Four... Three... Two... One...

The papers on the bedside table were scattered carelessly across the floor by the wind blowing in from the uncovered balcony. Walking slowly to the bed, he quickly took off his jacket and, hanging it on a chair, looked into the distance through the open balcony. He looked in the direction of where the bright crimson roof of the Langlais family mansion was visible during the day.

'Forgive me, Marie-Julie…' he whispered falling on the bed, and at the same instant fell asleep, exhausted.

He didn't dream again on that night.

'How about morning coffee in bed?'

Henri got up on his elbows trying to establish the source of the sound that had awakened him.

It was Jules hanging over him.

'I'd rather be asked about it by someone prettier,' he replied, rolling over onto his right side.

'Should I call the butler?' The younger man chuckled slyly, pulling the blanket off his brother.

'Call Miss France…' Henri snarled, burying himself in the pillow.

'What about the Moon Warrior Girls from your favorite girly anime? By the way, I heard that our father had certain fears at that time about you.'

'What ridiculous gender stereotypes? It's a cult classic of Japanese animation.' He yawned, taking away his blanket from Jules. 'Why so early? Isn't the burial scheduled for 11 am?'

'I had to postpone the burial until this evening. We need to be at a charity reception in Montparnasse by one o'clock so I'm expecting you for breakfast in twenty minutes,' the younger brother busily rapped out, and after waiting a few seconds added with a smile, 'monsieur emo bangs.'

Launching a pillow at his brother as he slipped through the door, Henri then stared motionlessly at the white ceiling for a few more minutes, realizing that for the first time in nineteen years he was sleeping within the walls of his HOME.

After taking a shower, getting dressed, and hastily dealing with breakfast, he sleepily got into the car. Having slept almost all the way, he suddenly found himself in the fifteenth arrondissement of Paris, or more precisely, in one of Europe's highest panoramic meeting rooms of the famous Montparnasse Tower.

Such events often reminded Henri of schooling fish. Clouds of them gathering together overcoming their insignificance in a desperate attempt to appear before the world as something more than themselves. All these noble guests, one by one swelled to incredible sizes by pouring liters of alcohol into the remnants of their minds from the very morning… Why did Jules bring him here right after breakfast? He still needed to have time to pack his suitcase before leaving. Henri turned to the clock nervously. It was just 13:20. Thus, he had about ten and a half hours before the return flight to Hong Kong. In general, that was enough.

'Well, Mr. Clairvoyant,' the youngest of Lero's children interrupted his thoughts, nonchalantly sipping his orange juice. 'Who appears before your eyes this time?'

'Judging by the people gathered today…' Henri lazily moved his gaze around the room, slightly lingering on an interesting figure distantly drinking a cocktail at the entrance, 'a flock of zander.'

'Zander fish?' The blond bit his lower lip with a question. 'Explain.'

'They live only in freshwater,' Henri began, pointing emphatically at the press huddled in the corner. 'Otherwise, they wouldn't be shining on the camera. Predators. They are betrayed by the large canine teeth on the upper and lower jaws,' he continued, glancing around at the personal bodyguards who were on duty along the perimeter of the hall. 'Judging by the visible signs' – he looked from guest to guest, mentally highlighting individual items of their wardrobe – 'their diet mainly consists of small fish, frogs or crayfish.' Catching the bewildered look of his interlocutor, he immediately took the trouble to explain. 'They are mainly nourished by the middle classes.' Taking a bite of an olive from a glass, he continued, 'Remind me of the main theme of today's reception.'

'Inauguration of the Fund for Fighting Corruption in Eastern Europe and Central Asia,' Jules said with interest.

'Well, of course… They prefer a pebble bottom, especially if there are driftwood, stumps, and stones behind which they can hide. They use them as a shelter.' Henri pointedly looked at the sign with the foundation's logo. 'This behavior helps fish to hunt from an ambush. The color allows zander to camouflage, so they can come very close to their prey and then they grab their quarry with a sharp jerk. Most of them must be bankers or sales representatives.

So... Why am I here? I have a flight back at half-past eleven tonight,' he drawled lazily.

'Wait a couple more minutes, brother.' The blond man snapped tenderly. 'Just try not to eat anyone here,' he added, patting Henri on the shoulder. 'I'll go find a couple of people and come back with news; with good news I hope.'

Henri gazed thoughtfully into the corner, not taking his eyes off the male silhouette that interested him at the very entrance.

'But what's more interesting,' he continued in a whisper, 'although zander is considered a schooling predatory fish, nevertheless, its largest individuals prefer solitude.' He finished, having dealt with the olive and removed the still full glass of Margarita on the next table, before heading directly toward the tall stranger. 'Broad-shouldered...' He noted.

Broad shoulders have always subconsciously aroused admiration in Henri. Firstly, because as he often liked to repeat his earthly idol, aunt Selena, nothing so clearly indicates the strength of a man's character as majestic shoulders and back. Secondly, he, unfortunately, did not possess all this. Despite his honorary thirty-three years, he was still much smaller than his own younger brother.

'Do we know each other?' said the man in bewilderment as he slowly sipped his "Maytai," desperately trying to figure out why the dark-haired stranger had come so close, and had been staring at silently him for a full one and a half minutes.

'Oh, I'm sorry,' emerging from the depths of his thoughts, Henri answered. 'Henri Lero,' he added, holding out his hand. 'My brother Jules is one of the owners of this building. This hall is, of course, not the Louvre, but as they say...' Henri's eyes treacherously jumped down on the incredibly beautiful graceful wrists, gently wrapped around the strong arms of the "zander."

'Gerald, my friend, will you introduce me to your interlocutor?' Henri, with difficulty, shifted his gaze from the stunning girlish brows to the abyss-like dark eyes. Without a doubt, if the broad-shouldered one was a zander, then she must be the sea ooze. Definitely! If the fall into infinity really had a bottom, then in the darkness, when you finally reached that ocean bed of ooze, you would sacrifice any moral position you ever had without a twinge of conscience. Unique in nature, this creation includes tens thousands of plants, on the throne of the numerical advantage of which algae invariably sit. First, she will give you everything you desire, and then only she will become all that you need.

'Monsieur Lero, let me introduce you to my boss. Mademoiselle Mila Crule,' the "zander" said reluctantly, in a rather irritated voice. He did not enjoy this conversation.

'Mila Nicole Crule,' she corrected with a smile. 'Lero…' The woman pointedly bit her lower lip. 'I heard about your father; my condolences. A very unpleasant story. An accident in broad daylight.' The girl looked down tragically in a theatrical manner. 'And also about your brother… He was pretty good in the post of "Head of the house,"' she finished with a shaking his hand gently.

'Thank you, mademoiselle. Thomas was a worthy replacement for my father, and not only about the settlement of internal affairs' – Henri paused for a moment – 'but also in the development of new directions. In which, I would venture to assume, after just a few years, the company could become a leader.' He raised his right eyebrow looking straight into the bottomless eyes, opposite him. 'I would call his leadership style impeccable,' he concluded in a very formal tone, not taking his eyes off the girl. 'Once again, thank you, and glad to meet you, Mademoiselle Crule. The heir to the legendary Crule Empire… Our ancestors once had a common business interest, if I'm not mistaken?' he added, freeing his hand from the gentle touch of such a gentle ooze.

'Yes, I suppose you're right.' Mademoiselle Crule snapped shortly, taking a small sip of her piña colada and shifting the cocktail glass to her now free right hand. 'But your ancestor overtook mine by playing a friendship to death with a bunch of voodoo fans somewhere in Africa,' she added sarcastically.

That was some reaction… 'Well, Queen, have you been offended by my innocent question?' Smiling blissfully, Henri mentally repeated to himself, not taking his eyes off her. Capriciously knitted eyebrows, twitching a slightly stray strand from the face…

"It's not the whole truth, Mademoiselle Crule," he drawled with a smile.

'What is he talking about?' Angrily squeezed out the heated "zander."

'Mademoiselle Crule knows what.' Gently releasing the glass from her hand, Henri took it in his right hand and drank slowly. 'Not bad, but I've tried better,' he added smiling.

'Pardon, I need a moment of your attention,' interrupted the impeccable Jules. 'Dear friends, on behalf of our gallery, I would like to once again thank all those present at this important reception, especially the organizer of this event and…my charming bride to be… Mademoiselle Mila Nicole Crule!' The audience applauded and Mademoiselle Crule, a satisfied smile spreading across her face, grabbed her glass from the dumbfounded Henri and went up to the stage.

Henri still could not believe what was happening… 'Jules…what is he doing? Marrying the main competitor? But why!'

Meanwhile, Mademoiselle Crule quickly snatched the microphone from Jules. 'Dear friends, I am so glad to see you all today. I want to share my happiness with all three hundred of my best friends here.' The audience immediately reacted to the joke. 'Our wedding will become a truly historic event… After all, we will not just tie our destinies…' A whisper immediately filled the hall. 'Yes, you are all right. Exactly thirteen days from now, we will make a merger not only of our hearts but also of all our assets. In other words, between the East End Investment Company and the Octave Trust Fund there will be nothing private.' The audience burst into applause.

Henri coughed nervously… Nothing private… She means… He translated a serious look at Jules and understood everything… Trust Fund! Thirteen days… Jules will get up on the chessboard in place of Thomas… Henri pulled out of his pocket the boarding pass for the flight from Paris to Hong Kong that he'd carefully printed that morning. He crumpled it carelessly and then drank a volley of "Long Island" he'd taken from the tray of a passing waiter. Thirteen days… They only have thirteen days to win this game. His eyes raced convulsively through the hall, and his neckerchief suddenly began to choke him.

Freeing his neck a little, Henri put the glass on the next table and ran his hand through his well-styled hair, closed his eyes, and took a deep breath. One… Two… Three… Four… Five… Six… Seven… Eight… Opening his eyes, he felt different. The voices around him had died down, his heart had settled back into its normal rhythm. *Well*, he thought happily, *in any situation, you just need to calm down first and then...* And then his heart stopped. Directly in front of him, just ten meters away, a short, bronze-skinned lady in an elegant white dress and beige pumps with low heels was smiling at him in a friendly way. The same bronze skinned lady who he so often saw in his dreams. The bronze skinned girl whose lifeless body he found in her bedroom at Langlaist's house nineteen years ago… The same…but…alive! Marie-Julie…

'White walls... Walls... No, first the ceiling.' Henri frantically tried to bring his head, that was stubbornly refusing to obey him into a familiar state. Rising a little, he glanced at the bedside clock. Ten minutes to nine in the morning... Morning? He could remember nothing of how he got home, or what happened after 3 pm yesterday.

'I demand at least ten thousand euros for moral damage,' Jules, who appeared at the door, began offended.

'Did I host a silent movie night?' Henri suggested with an innocent smile.

'You think too well of yourself,' his younger brother replied in a censorious tone. 'In general, you have to dry-clean my suit, partially repair one of our Charentes lambics, and replace the chandelier in the common room. It cannot be repaired, I guarantee.'

'So Leopold returned...' Henri started with surprise. 'I suppose that the burial was moved again?'

'Yes, we have forty minutes to get to the cemetery. Who is Leopold?'

'Never mind. Jules, are you still good at racing on rusty bikes?' Henri asked his brother with raising his left eyebrow and with a challenge in his voice.

'And you still don't know how to lose?' the blond said sarcastically.

'You only ever overtook me a couple of times, so I would say that our chances are about equal now,' he said, getting up and pulling on his trousers and a turquoise sweatshirt emblazoned with the motif, M31.

'You wanted to say almost every time?' shouted Jules, already running down the stairs.

Jumping out into the courtyard, the brothers enthusiastically rushed to the old barn opposite the extension with the summer kitchen. To their surprise, the battered bicycles still supported the weight of an adult rider and even accelerated to pretty decent speeds. They were saddened only by the fact that the road near the house was very sticky. The rain that had begun at about six in the morning was still drizzling, making their path more and more like that childhood fatal escape in their father's car.

After cycling about five kilometers along the main road, they turned north. Having covered another three kilometers to drive to the grove, Henri and Jules finally approached the old family cemetery. This land had belonged to the Lero family since the time of purchase by their legendary founder-ancestor, Carl-Louis Lero, so the question where relatives would be buried has never been raised. Even if you were in the mood for cremation, be sure your ashes would be scattered around here somewhere. There are no other options.

Having parked their iron horses by the fence, the guys cautiously made their way to the graves through a small garden also belonging to the house of Lero.

'How much space…' Henri began admiringly. 'I still can't get used to it after Hong Kong.'

'You aren't thinking of putting a couple of forty-foot containers in here and turning them into a capsule hotel, are you?' quipped Jules with a smile stretched across his face.

'Well, of course, you'd like that, but for your information, I have long dreamed of opening my "jjimjibang." Just imagine your five-story Korean-style bathhouse, one with a night of playing Go and eating baked eggs,' Henri replied dreamily, vividly depicting him rolling an imaginary baked egg on the floor.

'Even if you don't mean a hundred-year-old egg,' the younger one responded with horror recalling his last trip to Guangzhou.

'Oh, it's good that you remember! I brought you seven packs of peppery chicken feet,' Henri suddenly said with a predatory smile.

'Thank you, dear brother. After all, I just adored them,' he said, covering his mouth with his palm, suppressing the gagging that appeared at the mere mention of these "favorite treats." And why did he just agree to that dispute with Henri during his last visit to Guangzhou?

'Good morning, gentlemen,' said the holy father, who was waiting to conduct the service for Thomas's interment.

'Good morning, Father Nicholas,' the heirs of the House of Lero greeted him with one voice.

'There are only ten minutes left before the burial, but I don't see anyone here except you two and the representatives from the funeral home.'

'It's all right, Father Nicholas. Most of the friends managed to say goodbye to the deceased yesterday, so it's just the close family for the burial service,' Jules responded, inviting the others to approach his brother's grave.

An interesting feature of this cemetery is that here you will not find the familiar sort of tombstones or statues of the dead. Instead, according to family tradition, the deceased were buried in wooden coffins made of Tronsoy oak (the same one from which the barrels are made, in which the cognac is aged).

Instead of a gravestone over the head of the deceased, a sapling is planted so that by the number of trees in this zone you can fairly accurately count the number of members of the Lero family buried here. The plan for the location of the graves was kept by the representatives of the funeral home, with whom the family had been doing business for the last two hundred years, and by the eldest heir of the house.

'Hello…' whispered Henri stopping near the flowering violet tree.

'Hi, Mommy,' Jules responded tenderly placing his hand on a dangling violet branch. 'Good afternoon, Father. Hello, uncle.' He immediately nodded toward the oak and poplar proudly towering nearby.

'I assume you settled on a maple?' Henri asked, turning in the direction of Thomas's grave.

'But that's not all,' he replied, pulling his brother by the sleeve. 'Do you see these seedlings?' He pointed in the direction of the barely noticeable seedlings around the grave. 'There will be lilies of the valley here next spring. He always loved them.'

'It's funny… I don't even know what flowers you prefer,' Henri drawled absently looking at the coffin standing opposite. He didn't want to bring up the conversation about yesterday's reception until evening, but still, he couldn't contain himself.

'If everything goes well, then I hope that for a very long time and you will not need this information.'

"If you wanted to strongly motivate yourself in this way to deal with all this family poltergeist nonsense, then I don't want to argue with you, because your motivation is clearly very strong." Henri chuckled. 'But thirteen days…' He breathed heavily. 'I can't believe that my little Guppy is going to fight most of the ocean. Mind you, I do not even name who specifically, because I have no idea about who or what we are talking about.'

'Well, I have a significant advantage in this game,' Jules whispered mysteriously.

'What's the advantage?' Henri asked puzzled, knitting his eyebrows and turning his head to the younger man.

'You,' Jules replied with a smile, putting his hand on Henri's shoulder.

'Everything is even worse than I thought,' Henri said, hysterically shuddering with laughter and immediately catching a stern look from the Holy Father, who had already begun the funeral service.

'By the way, about the engagement...' Henri continued in a whisper. 'You could find a nicer contender.'

'Come on! Are you serious?' Jules demanded. 'As for her character – I won't argue, but what about her appearance?'

'It's just a nightmare,' scoffed Henri. 'I didn't see anyone uglier that evening.'

Jules poked his brother in the stomach, shaking with laughter.

The Holy Father made a gesture and coming closer, the guys put their palms on the lid of the coffin for the last time, after which the funeral home workers began to lower it into the grave. 'I... I should have been lying there. I, not Thomas,' Henri said, his thoughts spinning.

'Are you okay?' asked Jules, looking concerned.

'Yes, just... Too much for just two days. You know, you almost killed me with your engagement news yesterday. I...' Henri hesitated. 'I even started imagining some crazy stuff,' he said, rubbing his temples.

'What kind of stuff?' Jules asked, seriously.

'Well...' Henri let out a slow breath, 'do you remember Marie-Julie? One of the Langulet twins. She was three years older than me.'

'Yes of course. They were our closest neighbors.'

'It seemed to me that I saw her at the reception...alive,' Henri said nervously rubbing his hands.

'In what sense do you mean alive? Henri, did you confuse anyone with her, or are you surprised that you saw a live girl who was still alive at our reception?' he asked, smiling.

Henri froze, unable to move. That is... How is it...alive?

'Jules... we were pretty close with her in our school years.'

'By the way, not only with her,' Jules interrupted him reproachfully.

'Yes, but...that night when we left the house... Do you remember how we drove to the Langulet's house?'

'I remember that we stayed somewhere near our house, but nothing more.'

'She had severe depression in those years, after the death of their mother. Just like...just like ours. I know there was something else, something that she couldn't share with me. Or maybe I didn't want to listen to her. I don't remember. In general, that evening I wanted to say goodbye to her before leaving. Out of habit, going into the house from the kitchen, I went up to the second floor and... I... I...' Henri began to stutter. 'She... I found her with cut veins laying on her bed,' he continued squatting down and covering his head with his hands. When I realized that she wasn't breathing… I just…I just ran away… I ran away like a miserable coward.'

'Henri, listen… I understand that I shouldn't ask you about this, but… I've never heard about it from anyone. Plus, our father said that at that time you… In general, are you sure that all this was real?'

'Yes…' Henri answered confidently, standing up. 'I promised our uncle that I would quit, and I quit smoking that filth the moment that I made him that promise.'

'Hmm…' Jules exhaled heavily. 'I haven't had much contact with anyone from Langulet lately, but I'm pretty sure the twins are still in good health, like their father. Thomas saw him about six months before the ceremony and during… During this ceremony… Perhaps the girl survived after a suicide attempt and the Langulet house simply didn't want it to come out.'

'Yes, but… She… I'm pretty sure… There was so much blood, and her eyes and skin.' Henri was taken aback. 'Sure… Probably you're right. It's just my nerves,' finished Henri, putting his hands in his pockets.

Approaching the coffin the brothers took a handful of earth in their hands and looking down for the last time said goodbye to Thomas.

Having reached the house in the pouring rain, they threw their bicycles down at the entrance, and hastily entered the house. Jules immediately went to have a shower and Henri was about to follow his brother's example, and had, in fact, already taken a couple of steps up the stairs toward his room, but his plans were interrupted by a deafening ringing.

'RING RRRINNG…' the old city phone growled menacingly at its owners through the entire living room.

Henri reluctantly picked up the phone.

'House of the Lero family, how can I help you?' he asked politely.

'Monsieur Lero, Good afternoon! This is your butler, François de Gallon.'

'Good afternoon, Monsieur de Gallon,' Henri said in surprise. 'Sorry, I didn't recognize your voice. I thought you had a day off, today. Maybe something happened?' he suggested.

'No, monsieur, everything is fine. I'm calling to inquire about your well-being. You weren't very well yesterday,' the butler replied with undisguised awkwardness in his voice.

Henri turned his gaze to the marble table and saw a fat cigarette butt in the ashtray.

'Monsieur de Gallon,' Henri interrupted, 'do you smoke?'

'No, sir. None of the staff at the house do.'

'It's commendable… Jules also doesn't smoke and I quit a week ago,' he drawled, puzzled. 'I beg your pardon for my unseemly appearance and thank you very much for your help, I suppose you and Jules weren't happy about having to drag me up to the second floor and undress me like a three-year-old child.'

'Oh, monsieur, your girlfriend took care of everything.'

'Girlfriend?' Henri couldn't believe his ears. Why couldn't he remember any of this at all?'

'Yes. A very courteous, beautiful, and very strong young lady. She helped you get to the bedroom, put you to bed, and left the house almost immediately. This all happened two hours before your brother arrived.'

His thoughts were swirling in a mad dance, circling inside Henri's head, not allowing him to build all this mess into a coherent logical series. There were only images and flashes in his head: Something gradually groping… Someone's hands, smile, blue car, then their house, his legs, floor, and lips… Lips? It seemed that it was a barely perceptible kiss on the top of his head. Henri was beginning to remember how she… She! Who is she? Come on, Henri, try to remember. He closed his eyes and mentally filled the room with water, trying to plunge into that very sleepy state. Women's hands covered him with a blanket, lips kissed the top of his head and whispered:

'Sleep tight… Sleep… Nasty emo boy.'

Those last words surfaced in his memory, electrifying him.

'Is everything all right, monsieur?' his butler, who was still on the line, asked him.

'I hope so, Monsieur de Gallon. I hope so…' Henri whispered, glancing at the lonely cigarette butt and looking at a large clock with a bronze octopus.

Chapter 3
Octopus

'Jules, now please explain it to me one more time,' Henri said, opening a glass bottle of mineral water. Henri leisurely began, swinging into the soft back of the passenger seat of the taxi. 'For what reason were we shaking in an airplane for almost seven hours to Dakar, if, as I noticed, if, we have been driving for a long time in the opposite direction from the main archive of the Trust?'

'If we can get into the lobby of the Dakar Pullman Hotel within the next ten minutes,' typing a text message, Jules replied, 'then, I believe, for the sake of meeting with Madame Ba…'

'Ba?' Henri raised his eyebrows in confusion. "I suppose that her surname before marriage was…"

'Kebe. That's correct. She's the guardian from the Kebe family, but for gender reasons, she was only temporary guardian of the Trust after the death of our father and until Thomas's inauguration. Now this position has passed to me.'

'But didn't Thomas sign documents before his death? In theory, you should be the Guardian regent, like our father after the death of an uncle.'

'Since he managed to leave only two signatures out of the four required, the volume of my powers is very limited. It equates my position with the Guardian of the Trust. Unfortunately, it's not enough to change something. That's why I decided to try all of this stuff with the marriage and inauguration. Go big…'

'…or go home. What about our tactic for negotiation?' Looking anxiously at the clock, Henri clarified when the minute shooter was already coming to half past twelve in the evening, Paris time, which meant they were almost late for the meeting.

'We'll try to get something from her reactions to the main versions of what's happening: it might be an external diversion, internal sabotage, or…'

'You don't think about it seriously, do you?' Henri looked at him skeptically.

'I saw what I saw and so did you. We can't rule out the "curse version." Plus three months ago they had a meeting with Thomas; she might know something about his death.'

'Sounds reasonable…'

The views of the coast from the windows of the car suddenly reminded Henri that he had not yet opened his swimming season this year. Firstly, he suffered from a heavy bout of flu in the spring, after that was a hold-up at work in connection with the launch of a new line after signing a big contract with a rather fat American company, and the final reason was the revision of old models for several international expos all at once. The Neuro market is still very young and rapidly gaining, so you need to constantly keep your finger on the pulse. Here you should keep working hard seven days a week from 8 a.m. to 9 pm… This happens when you are working on your product. Well, on your aunt's product, actually. Everything in the company belongs to her and Henri is just one of an infinite number of middle-level managers with a small team and a couple of his own developments.

'What a pity that we can't stay here for a couple of days,' Henri drawled dreamily.

'Yes, people are drawn to the ocean,' Jules confirmed with a smile.

'Pulls… Pulls back into the water,' the older man agreed, nodding.

'Monsieur Lero, we are now opposite the Pulman Hotel,' the driver reported in a bass voice.

'Thank you, Monsieur Géraud. Please park nearby. We should be free within an hour. I'll call you as soon as we're done,' Jules told him politely.

As soon as the car slowed down the young porter arrived immediately. He kindly escorted them to the main lobby of the hotel. The main hall with hazel color walls has no different from the lobbies of most chain hotels, which nowadays were scattered all over the world.

It's funny, Henri thought. *Day by day, year by year, we're all becoming more and more similar to each other. We laugh at the same videos on the Internet, eat the same food, translate foreign memes, sing the same songs, but for some reason, we can't become closer to each other. How many more years have to pass before we see unity as citizens of the Earth? Fifty? Two hundred? One thousand? Is humanity able to live in peace with itself?*

'What are you thinking about?' Jules asked with a smile, nudging his brother with his elbow. He pointed to the head waiter, who kindly invited them to go to the lounge bar for their meeting.

'I... I remembered the disgusting crooked hands of my future sister-in-law,' the elder brother answered sarcastically. 'My nephews... My poor nephews! They will have to wear hand braces to somehow remedy the situation.' Henri scoffed and immediately received a slight push to the left side from his younger brother. 'Hey, why? You said that it's a fake relationship.'

'If it wasn't fake, I would have done this.' Jules replied, giving Henri a painful pinch in his neck, a satisfied smile spreading across his face.

The table booked in their name was in the open part of the hotel bar, which overlooked the coast. There was no wind today and the sky was so clear that it opened a view of thousands stars.

'I hope the flight was not too tiring for you?' asked a stately lady heading toward them with almond-shaped brown eyes of incredible depth. A long chiffon dress of a delicate olive color favorably emphasized the dignity of her magnificent figure and her hair was wrapped in a pale peach shawl, that was matched in perfect harmony with the sandals of a lighter tone on her feet. She looked to be about fifty-five.

'Nice to finally meet you, Madame Ba,' Jules began, holding out his hand in greeting.

Henri was more old-fashioned, allowing himself to kiss the lady's hand, which fortunately did not bother her at all.

'I believe that you have come not only to admire this ocean or enjoy my company?' Madame Ba said with a smile, as she sipped her freshly squeezed orange juice.

'That's right, madam,' Henri began. 'We have only four questions: our grandfather, our father, our uncle, and finally our brother Thomas.'

'Upfront and honest... Well... I have only one answer for you: According to your faith be it unto you.'

'Madame Ba, we need your help with admission to the first records of the Trust fund. There is a possibility that we might find something useful,' Jules continued cautiously.

'But you have access to the archive of the Trust as temporary Guardian,' the woman answered with a frown.

'Yes, but... I'm talking about the first archive that belongs to your family.'

'What would you want to find there? A curse recipe?' she suggested laughing. 'I know that my great-grandfather could said something in the heat of the moment. I also know that he was hanging around with sorcerers, but he was not a sorcerer himself. Although... Curse or poison... Why do we need to talk about what happened hundreds of years ago?'

'Madame Ba, with all due respect, you and I are well aware of the benefits that the Trust brings to our families. We could blindly deny this obvious fact for a very long time until we sadly have to admit that both sides are equally interested in solving this puzzle,' Henri blurted out sharply.

'The same? Equally?' unable to bear it, the woman burst out. 'Equally interested? Perhaps I should remind you that as Monsieur Lero's former senior heir you disgracefully fled from this benefit? Or maybe I should remind you that it was your ancestors, not mine, who made a fortune by robbing my folk? Or should I remind you about your father, uncle, brother, or a dozen other members of the founding families who died under mysterious circumstances?'

'That's true, but victims were not only among the founding families...' Henri said confidently, seeing how the expression on her face slowly changed from anger to fear, 'and you know about it from your own experience. Even if you don't admit to yourself that you always knew the reason why...'

'Silence!' Madame Ba interrupted him rudely. 'You don't understand what you're talking about right now.' She stood up abruptly without finishing her juice.

'How many exclusively female heirs were in the Kebe family in recent years? Your grandfather, father, and your unborn son... What happened to them? This is what Thomas was trying to find out? Did you talk about that with him? Henri whispered, jumping to his feet and coming close to her.

Madame Ba jerked as if from a wasp sting and turned sharply toward the exit.

'Madam, wait!' Jules shouted after her. 'We're just trying to understand something. After all, Thomas...' He clenched his hand tightly into a fist. 'You knew him. Thomas was a very good man.' His voice suddenly trembled. 'He didn't deserve such a fate.'

Madame Ba stopped almost at the very exit and without turning said:

'The building on Kostel Street on the Goree Island. I will send the exact address of the archive in a message within ten minutes. I'll give you until five in the morning. The morning shift will arrive at six am, so you must be gone by half-past five. There's a lot of material and the path is not the nearest one, so I advise you to go there immediately. My man will meet you at the entrance to the building.'

'Thank you,' Jules whispered politely.

'Thank Thomas,' she said without turning around and disappeared through the door.

It took about forty minutes to reach Goree Island, where the Trust Custodians' family archive was located. The brothers barely made it in time for the last ferry and arrived on the island by midnight. Despite the late hour, there were quite a lot of people willing to take the two Frenchmen to the center. Choosing the driver who seemed most knowledgeable about the destination, they immediately hit the road.

'What a beautiful land!' whispered Henri, admiring the views of the night island. 'I can't believe that only three hundred years ago this island was a prison.'

'No one can, monsieur,' the driver agreed with him smiling, looking around the road. 'I've lived here as long as I can remember and I can't believe it, too.'

'The past should remain in the past,' Henri said with a smile.

'Always,' the young man agreed with a nod as he parked his car in front of a small two-story building near St. Charles's Catholic Church.

Having said goodbye to the driver the brothers slowly walked to the inconspicuous building that housed the archive. At the entrance, a smiling man in white trousers and a blue plaid shirt was waving good-naturedly to them.

"That's all?" Jules laughed. 'I expected to see a bunch of guards here, armored doors, one lock with a retinal scan, and a dozen shepherd dogs…'

'Sure, that's why you took with you a "karate kid" like me,' Henri quipped. 'We would have jumped out of the window during an explosion and then disappeared into the night on motorcycles. Did I tell you that in my youth I drove a rickshaw? I even had my own business in Guangzhou. I took tourists to the wholesale markets,' the elder brother continued proudly.

'You? In Guangzhou? No, you'd be taken to the police on the first day of illegal work. Mr. Blue-eye immigrant,' Jules said skeptically.

'No-no... People often confused me with the locals. Well, I seemed to look like a kid from a mixed marriage child, or one of the Uyghur folk.'

'Monsieur Lero.' Madame Ba's representative greeted them extending his hand for a handshake.

'Monsieur Nerp, nice to meet you. I'm Jules and this is my older brother, Henri.'

'Oh, you remind me of your uncle, Monsieur Henri. Especially your eyes, 'he observed with interest.

'Yes. Unfortunately, he left us just at my age...'

'My condolences... I had the honor to know your uncle, your father, and your brother... Thomas was a wonderful person with a smile from the heart.'

'Yes. He was. Thank you,' Henri replied with gratitude, patting him on the shoulder.

The first floor of the building was no different from a typical hotel or hostel on Goree Island. Light beige hall, a lot of space, and minimalism in furniture. Along the right wall, there were tall showcases with various utensils and ivory products from the trade of which the history of the guild began. All of this linked the families of the founders together.

Jules asked Monsieur Nerpa how to turn on the additional light on the first floor. To the left side of the entrance, Henri saw a large photo of the legendary founders of the Octave Trust and several other small portraits. He was looking at the faces in the photo with curiosity. The men in it wore simple but elegant suits with the same copper octopus brooch on the lapels of their jackets.

In the center of the photo was Monsieur Solomon Kebe – the first Guardian of the Trust. Solomon was unusually tall, almost two heads taller than Carl-Louis Lero, whose portrait Henri had seen thousands of times in his father's cabinet, and Lyon Langlais whose luxuriant family curls, and an exaggerated sense of his superiority, were inherited by a good many of his descendants, including their neighbor's twins, Marie-Julie and Charles Langlaist.

Not inferior to Solomon in size, an obese, chubby, and sullen man who strongly resembled a bear was most likely the founder of the Bernard House – Oberon Bernard. Henri's classmate Oberon was named after this man – this was the Oberon who died in a fire with his family three months ago.

'It's funny,' Henri whispered, looking into the man's face. 'The surname Bernard also means "bear."'

Next to Oberon in the photo was a very young, but very strong, man, whose white-toothed smile appeared two or three shades lighter than anything in this black and white photograph. Most likely, it was Christopher Aigle. Christopher, judging by his posture, was not very comfortable standing next to Oberon. These two men seemed to be trying to jostle each other, trying to take as much space in the frame as possible. It's interesting that, despite some external confrontation, these two somehow strongly resembled each other. Perhaps, from some vantage point, Henri could easily confuse them, but there was one big difference between them – the expressions on their faces.

To the left of Christopher in the photo were Castor Cartier and a short middle-aged man unknown to Henri, but most likely Anatole Cigogne. Not far from Lyon Langlaist, he noticed the serious face of the Maori Drago and the elongated face framed by the graceful mustache that belonged to Mario Loup.

All eight representatives of the founding families standing there in one photo, which indicated that it must have been taken in the period after 1973 when Hilderic Oak joined the Trust. Thus, our "Octopus" has exactly eight "tentacles."

'Henri, we're done here,' Jules said as he climbed the stairs. 'Let's go to the archive.'

The second floor of the archive represented some semblance of a cozy library. Ten tall racks stretched along a small hall measuring approximately fifteen by twenty meters. The archive had a small file, which indicated the location of rare family books, directories, brief archival records, and current affairs reports from the guild time until the foundation of the Trust.

'Sow many books...' Jules sighed hard. 'We just need to figure out a way to split ourselves into at least fifty people before 3 am and then we'll be able to finish work by five.'

'Let's focus on the main thing,' Henri said, discarding his beige jacket on a chair standing near the door. 'Half of the manuscripts here are fiscal year reports, ivory literature, or grape care. I'll take over the "Old Testament,"' he said, removing his cufflinks and rolling up the sleeves of his azure shirt above the elbow. Henri continued, 'Your task will be to check out all the summaries of the founding families from 1945. We should fix on some notes about bankruptcies, accidents...'

'Cattle pestilence, epidemics, and full moons.' Smiled Jules, who also rolled up his sleeves.

'Are you sure that this is your first attempt to remove the centuries-old curse from yourself and avoid an equally terrible marriage?' Henri whispered inquiringly, patting his brother on the shoulder and moving away toward the high shelves.

'It seems to me that someone here clearly fell for my future wife,' he mocked, as he moved away in the opposite direction.

'Monsieur Nerp, he said it about you,' retorted Henri, but judging by the fact that there was no answer, each of them was already busy with their own business. Jules pored over books and Monsieur Nerp went to take a nap on the first floor.

Having embarked on a search, Henri discovered that most of the "Old Testament" books and manuscripts were indeed devoted to the processing of ivory and the conduct of commercial affairs. The first records of the Guild as they called themselves in those days dated back to the middle of the fourteenth century when the distant ancestors of the Langlais, Lero, Bernard, Crule, Oak, and Loup families from Denier began their first attempts at trade on the coast of Gambia and Senegal.

The period from 1370 to 1413 could be called "golden" for the Guild because at that period numerous merchant ships arrived at the white rocks of Denier. This was until the outbreak of the Lancaster War. The war greatly influenced the affairs of the Guild, and this stage was marked by the separation of the main part of the guild from the Langlais family and the forced cessation of trade with Africa. With the departure of Langlais, a long period of the rise of the Lero family began. This period culminated in the restoration of trade ties with Senegal and even the opening of offices, first in Saint Louis and then on the Goree in the second half of the seventeenth century.

This lasted until 1783 when a young and ambitious Chuck Aisle joined the company. In 1803, the Langlais family returned to the Guild. At the beginning of the nineteenth century, the Guild was not only concerned with ivory but also textiles and the sale of medicines and peanuts.

From 1825, Lero insisted on actively investing in the development of railways, which allowed the Guild to begin producing gold and cotton. In 1880, the Oak clan inexplicably left the guild and in 1882, it was joined by the Loup and Crule families. By the way, the current head of the Crule House is going to be Jule's wife in just 13 days.

So, on the one hand, we have Langlais, Lero, and Bernard, and on the other, Oak, Loup, and Crule. In 1907, the union of Léreaux, Langlais, and Bernarda was joined by Aigle and in 1915 the Oak, Loup and Crule clan was joined by the Deminor family. The wife of Enver Damour Aremi was the subject of exhalation for Boris Bernard and the object of abuse for her husband. In one diary, Henri read about a case where Enver beat his wife so badly that a local doctor was forced to spend three nights at her bedside fighting for her life. After this Boris Bernard came to their house demanding a duel and revenge for the evil that had been done. The conflict was resolved peacefully, but in 1917 under mysterious circumstances, the Head of the Bernards clan died, and a year later, in 1918, that fate led to the collapse of the head of the Oaks House. In 1919, the House's leaders signed an agreement to jointly develop new trade destinations and in 1933, they were joined by the House of Cartier, presented by the young Castor Cartier. In 1940, Loup and Oak exited the Guild and joined in open competition with the Bernards. In 1941, the Aigle family had a new competitor in the person of Anatol Cigogne.

The difficult economic situation along with World War II practically puts an end to the Guild's affairs, but in 1945, the Heads of the Houses found the strength and desire to forget former grievances for the sake of a common future. At that time, a five families' Trust fund was established.

The heads of the Trust were the five founding families: Langlais, Lero, Aigle, Cartier, and Bernard, and a little later the Drago house joined them. Then, in 1955, they were joined first by the Loup house, in 1956 by the Cigogne family, and in 1973 by the Oak clan. In 1956, the Trust was renamed "Octave" and received a coat of arms in the form of an octopus.

Since its inception, the Trust fund had been managed by Solomon Kebe, whose family has been a reliable trading partner of the guild for many years and helped keep it afloat during wartime.

'Monsieur Leroy, we have only ten minutes left.' The voice of Monsieur Nerpa interrupted the train of Henri's thoughts.

'Thanks. I've already finished everything. Henri, how about you?'

'Okay, we can go,' Henri muttered a little bewilderedly at the clock that showed four hours and twenty minutes in the morning.

Stretching in their crumpled clothes, the brothers, tired but satisfied with the work done, went out into the yard. A full day reigned on the street, but it was empty just now. Monsieur Nerp volunteered to give the brothers a lift to the ferry, for which the guys, who were half asleep, were ready to kiss him. Monsieur Nerp just smiled politely, saying that he could not have done otherwise for the Thomas's brothers.

The road was smooth and Jules without thinking twice decided to take a nap on the way. It can be rather comfortable if you keep the speed to about 30–35 kilometers per hour. This way for this business, he had about 15–20 minutes.

Henri leaning back in his seat admired the views of the morning Goree and replayed in his head the events from the charity reception in the Montparnasse tower:

'If Jules is right and I saw Marie-Julie alive that evening, then judging by the words of the butler, it was she who drove me home on the evening of the reception and put me to bed. And this after I left her to die… No wonder that when she laid me down, she finally called me a nasty emo boy, just as her twitchy brother Charles once called me. Hmmm… But why was she babysitting me that evening?' Henri looked at the sleeping Jules and smiled slightly. The main thing was that they were still alive and had more information about what's happening than a day ago.

The silence was broken by a phone call.

'Monsieur Lero,' the caller addressed him in a hoarse voice. 'It's Monsieur Shiraz from the private boarding school named after Saint Ichtis.'

'Good morning, Monsieur Shiraz. How are you?'

'Oh, thank you, Monsieur Lero, everything is fine. I'm calling at the request of a friend of yours regarding our records about Marie-Julie Langlaist.'

'Do you have anything?' asked Henri, diligently holding back the tremor rising to his throat. Only a few seconds separated him from the truth. Marie-Julie's life at the moment was like Schrödinger's cat. She was both alive and dead at the same time, which is why his heart was beating furiously, realizing how important these few seconds were now.

'Yes, Monsieur Lero. I hasten to inform you that there were no abnormal events in the education of Mademoiselle Langlais. She graduated from the boarding house with honors and even won a scholarship to study at Cambridge.'

'Oh, it's…' – Henri hesitated – 'a little bit unexpected for Mademoiselle Langlais. She didn't always do so well in her studies… But I am extremely happy about this call,' Henri whispered, finally inhaling deeply.

'Yes, Mademoiselle Langlais has changed a lot since that autumn, when her twin brother Charles suddenly left the boarding house and moved to relatives in Seoul.'

'That autumn… Was it nineteen years ago?' barely holding the phone in a trembling hand, Henri asked.

'Yes… Well, since you know, I dare not bother you anymore, Monsieur Lero. I will send you the files by mail. Say hello to Monsieur Jules,' Monsieur Shiraz whispered benevolently, hanging up.

The car had already pulled up to the port when a sharp slap on the shoulder from his brother brought Henri out of shock.

'Well, Henri, to Dakar and back to Paris?' the younger man asked with a smile, pointing in the direction of the ferry ticket office.

'My little Guppy is marrying only once, so don't think you can get away from the bachelor party. A bachelor party in Seoul.' Henri finished putting his hand on his brother's shoulder.

'I have a bad feeling,' Jules said looking into the distance through the windshield.

'Yes… Me too,' agreed Henri and leaning back in the seat absentmindedly looked into the distance, too.

Chapter 4
The Crane Fish

The flight to Seoul gave the brothers a fifteen-hour respite in which they were finally able to organize the information they had received and even taken a nap. The clock during passport control was already showing at twenty minutes to two Paris time, which made them rush to get into the taxi since the meeting with Henri's friend was scheduled in the bustling student district of Hongdae an hour before midnight local time.

Despite the rather busy metropolitan traffic, they arrived at the appointed barbecue restaurant a little ahead of schedule, which greatly delighted Henri, who was raging for a glass of soju.

'It's a strategic success,' he whispered, busily ordering several types of meat and grills in poor Korean.

'Why are you so pleased?' Jules looked attentively at him narrowing his eyes. 'We're on a double date or what?' he added with a cough, and grimaced slightly at the unexpectedly strong pomegranate soju.

'It's better! Today, dear brother, I will finally introduce you to my best friend. Jiwon and I have known each other for fifteen years, if not more.' He continued tapping on the menu.

'That's the famous Doctor Bak?' Jules raised his eyebrows.

'She's the Legendary Dr. Bak.' The elder brother stretched out his hand, giving the menu to the waiter. '년은 당신을 아끼지 않았다 (years have not been merciful to you),' he suddenly shouted to someone near the entrance.

'너 자신은 오래된 걸레처럼 보인다 (and you look like an old rag),' said a tall curly-haired Korean woman with an asymmetrical bob who had just entered the restaurant.

According to Henri's words, Bak Jiwon must be around 36 years old, but she looked much younger. A thin menthol cigarette was smoking in the girl's left hand, while with her right she was carefully adjusting her stylish round glasses with silver frames. Despite the rather cool autumn evening, she was dressed quite lightly. Green windbreaker with a tiger embroidered on the right sleeve, over a white T-shirt, black cotton breeches, and slates on bare feet.

Jules, who didn't understand what was going on, intuitively recognized Jiwon in the girl who entered, and immediately politely extended his hand to her to make her acquaintance.

'Glad to finally meet my older brother's best friend, Dr. Bak.'

'You too. Mr. Lero. Does this weirdo persist in calling me his best friend?' she asked looking at Henri. 'I've only known him for two weeks.'

'Yes? Then who did this?' asked Henri, rolling up his left sleeve and pointing to an oblong scar.

'Uh-uh-uh... I didn't think you were dumb enough to jump there.' Jiwon hissed, raising her eyebrows threateningly. 'Seven years have passed. I've told you many times, let's draw a line under that.'

'Not for free, by the way. Spared money for her best friend!' Henri complained to his brother.

'씨꽐 (badass)... I'll put a second one on you for symmetry,' said Jiwon clutching Henri's right hand and pinching his side in parallel.

'救命! 救命! (Help me! Help me!),' he shouted in bad Chinese, causing bewilderment among the rest of the barbecue visitors. Dr. Bak immediately rushed to react, apologizing to the visitors and explaining that her French friend just found out he missed two rallies in Paris and got upset about that. Jiwon's comment first prompted a flurry of howling, and then an understanding nod to everyone present.

'So,' Henri began, 'the situation is this: we have two brothers, one cursed, eight primary suspects from the Founding families, and 193 people if we take into account all the minor beneficiaries of the Trust. By the "curse," we mean the deaths of seven Heads of the Founding Families, who temporarily assumed the powers of the Guardians, and the death of several direct heirs of the Foundation Guardians through the Kebe line. Now let's go through the deaths chronologically.' He diligently sketched all the key aspects of the problem on a napkin.

-1945: Oak and Cigogne tried to become the main managers of the Trust behind everyone's back. For this, they were cursed by Solomon Kebe, who knew the famous sorcerer on the Goree, and there you are – within two months, they died. Their deaths are described as painful. Unfortunately, there are no details.

-1979: Solomon Kebe himself died in a car accident. The Head of Aigle House takes over the powers of Solomon and dies on the evening of initiation, exactly at midnight. The description looks like poison or a heart attack. There are several records and they all differ. Control passes to his widow.

-1989: The head of the Bernards House wanted to take over the right of control, but the outcome was the same as in previous cases. Death also occurred at midnight. Control passes to Bernard's widow.

-1996: Our grandfather intended to take control… Henri hesitated. His death came exactly at midnight, from symptoms… Foam from the mouth, severe convulsions, and blood from the eyes. Management passes to the temporary regent, which became our grandmother.

-2000: Henri's voice faltered. 'After the sudden death of his grandmother, his father and uncle decided not to share this information with outsiders. They announced her death only the evening before the initiation, so this way none of the other families had any time to decide which of their own they would send to the slaughter. Symptoms…' He took a deep breath. 'The symptoms were the same and the time… Exactly at midnight. Since the uncle did not have a wife, his confidant was his father, who assumed temporary management as regent. So it lasted seven years before the Trust was managed by the grown heir from the Kebe family – young Nicholas Kebe. Nicholas safely handled his role right up until late last year, when he died of a heart attack. Temporary management was transferred to his older sister, Madame Ba. For an incomprehensible reason in recent years, all-male heirs who were born into both Nicholas's family and his sister's family did not survive, they were miscarried.'

'Quite a good match for the Heads of the Founding families.' Jiwon observed while roasting the meat.

'We think that these "coincidences" were the main reason for Madame Ba's reluctance to talk about the events.' Henri stretched thoughtfully. 'We found Thomas's records about the series of miscarriages in the Kebe family starting from 1990. Nicholas was born in 1989. He was the last one not touched by this terrible trend. So after his death, the place had to be taken by someone from the Founding families.' Henri looked in his glass of soju, unable to continue.

'2019: Thomas... The symptoms are absolutely the same as in the case with our grandfather and uncle,' Jules continued for him.

'Yes...' Henri confirmed. 'All, except the time. When all this happened to Thomas, it was only five minutes to midnight. I hardly believe that the "curse" could have rushed the sentence. It wasn't an accident...

'Thus, the circle of suspects is narrowed to representatives of eight Founding families. It's not possible that any of the other 50 beneficiary families know the details of the "curse." After all, to simulate all this so cleverly a lot of information is needed,' Jules continued turning to Jiwon. 'We assume that Thomas somehow managed to catalyze the process, by knocking his death out of the "curse" schedule by exactly five minutes.'

'Plus, during a trip to Goree we managed to learn that the general trend toward mysterious deaths under strange circumstances of the founding families was visible long before the foundation of the Trust. So the key question is not what is happening, but rather who is doing it?' explained Henri.

'And how?' Jules added, wiping his lips.

'Yes, and how?' the elder said thoughtfully. 'I forgot to mention that the Bernard family, they...were all burned to death, in full force three months before Thomas's initiation...'

'Well...' Jiwon began, pulling out the folders. 'I have three items of news for you: bad, worse, and almost good. Where to start?'

'With the bad one,' the brothers answered in unison.

'I managed to find out the current location of Charles Langlais. The bad news is that he is now in a Seoul Mental Hospital, and even worse, visitors are not allowed to visit him even for a minute's conversation. The almost good news is that I can still help Henri talk to him.'

'But it's great! Why, then, is this news almost good?' Jules asked, raising his eyebrows.

'Most likely, because they will put me there as a patient,' Henri said without blinking and draining another pile of soju in one gulp.

Jules looked in bewilderment from Henri to the smiling Jiwon.

'We will pick him up discreetly on the same day. A friend of mine promised to arrange everything. His man will look after you there.'

'Nice. I also wanted to find time for a sanatorium,' the elder Lero said, cutting the meat with his tongs. 'By the way, thanks. If you didn't help to request an extract from the boarding school, it's unlikely that we would have been able to catch on to the fact that all one hundred percent of the Langelet family's profits were transferred to Marie-Julie just six months before Thomas's inauguration.'

'Request? Boarding School?' Jiwon raised an eyebrow in disbelief.

'Then...' Henri drawled thoughtfully. 'That call...'

'Give me the number. I'll check everything through my guys,' Dr. Bak responded immediately.

'Please check the calls to our landline telephone in Paris. Something tells me that it was not our butler who called me recently.'

'You mentioned Marie-Julie. Isn't that THOSE girl?' Jiwon asked carefully.

'Yes. By the way, I'm almost sure that she's alive.'

'Almost sure?' widening her eyes in shock, Dr. Bak said. 'We need to get drunk!'

The dinner turned out to be funny and very hearty. Having finished their meal, the company moved toward the main street to catch a taxi and go home, but not even five meters away, Henri grappled with a passing promoter dressed as a large white cat. He borrowed the huge white cat's head and played a couple of bass lines in it along with the street musicians who had gathered a crowd nearby.

'What a shame!' Jules lamented. 'How much did he drink? Henri, what are you doing? Let's go to the hotel. You need to sleep. Hey, somebody's going to the psychiatric hospital tomorrow morning!' the youngest grumbled, spreading his arms to the sides.

At this time, satisfied, Dr. Bak stuck out her tongue with pleasure and enthusiastically recorded everything that was happening on the phone camera.

'Well, now he's finally here, let me introduce to you someone,' she explained nodding toward the raging Henri. 'This is my best friend Leopold.'

Dr. Bak was always distinguished by punctuality. She didn't like to wait. She really, really did not like waiting, but life loves irony, and therefore that very vile quality that she so fiercely hated both in her patients and people was ninety percent of all the habits of her best friend. Even the first time they met in Hong Kong, when she was returning to her dorm late in the evening from summer medical courses and saw a skinny, pale foreign boy surrounded by a gang of local bandits, she even then realized that this kid was a very problematic guy. For a split second, the postulates of Darwin's theory of natural selection flashed through her head, but her hand, obeying the call of her conscience, mechanically pulled the medical scalpel out of her backpack. She perfectly understood that she could not pass by.

Having interceded for him then, many years ago, she had doomed herself to friendship with this harmful boy, who later became practically her younger brother, and who more than once helped her and her family cope with grief, and to overcome difficulties. And even if fate spread them on different sides of the earth, like everything eternal, their true friendship had no expiration date.

'Good morning! Who ordered the smelly tofu?' Jules whispered cheerfully, opening the passenger door of an old KIA and carefully helping Henri to sit down in it, still suffering from a morning hangover.

'Oooh…' Jiwon drawled, turning her head toward the passenger seats. 'I would even say a thousand-year-old egg. Make sure you don't throw up in the car.'

'I'll try, Mom,' Henri quipped, sarcastically. 'Why am I not in the child seat?'

'Children in Korea are smaller. You wouldn't fit into a local child seat,' Jules answered, flipping through the news feed on his phone with one hand and fastening his seat belt with the other. Jiwon was meanwhile answering the phone.

'South Koreans have grown by ten centimeters over the past fifty years. Globalization makes us more and more identical to each other year after year. So I would venture to assume that in about five thousand years we will all be about 210 centimeters tall. We will have one, most likely, very specific skin tone that protects us from radiation. Plus we will have a small head.'

'Small?' Jules raised his left eyebrow in bewilderment.

'Yes, like human progress in big data compression, our brain will learn to work more compactly within the space allotted to it. Unnecessary areas will atrophy, the quality of brain cells will increase, and the speed of information processing will increase.'

'Descendants of Napoleon, we have a briefing,' Jiwon began as she drove away from the hotel building. 'The hospital is located in the suburb of Gwangju. It's about two hours from here. We registered you under the name Emmanuelle Sartre. You officially should stay there for three months. The diagnosis is mild bipolar disorder. Briefly about the biography: you are a literary critic, a creative person with all the ensuing consequences. Divorced, have a son,

Arthur. Your son is ten years old; he is studying at the St. Augustus boarding school in Paris. After the divorce, you got a pug named Kimchi. You come very often to Seoul for work. You are often on the road – this ruined your marriage. You are a vegetarian who's practicing hatha yoga. Your musical tastes: a big fan of Korean band Bandjuo and David Bowie.'

'I hope that I'm finally the only child in the family?' Henri clarified, for what immediately got a push in the side from Jules.

'Yes. Registration of patients in the hospital is until eleven in the morning, then you will be taken to the ward. Standard mode: wake up at seven in the morning, then personal time until nine. At nine in the morning, the morning round begins, followed by medication and breakfast. From ten-thirty to two in the afternoon, patients have visits to doctors, treatment workshops, and free time. From two to three, lunch and pills. From three to five, quiet hours in the wards, you can stay awake, but it is forbidden to leave the rooms. Dinner and medication at six in the evening. Art therapy takes place from seven o'clock to nine in the evening. At nine on the schedule, drugs and injections. And finally, at ten in the evening, the official lights out. Langlais should be kept on the fourth floor. Unfortunately, that's all that I can say now.

'The main thing is that it's not on the second floor,' Jules said with a smile and added, 'Room 217.'

'It's not a hotel,' Henri replied in a serious tone.

'But it still looks very similar,' insisted the younger.

'Not at all,' Henri continued indifferently. 'Reading horror books has developed your imagination too well.'

'The name of his man is Kim Litok. He said that the messenger will find you and that you will need to follow the "crane." You will have a little less than a day for everything. Today at midnight, the messenger will be waiting for you at the entrance to the kitchen, from where this "crane" will take you outside and bring you to Seoul. Any questions?' Jiwon looked at Henri through the driver's mirror; she looked extremely serious.

'Phones, communication?' specified Henri.

'Complete isolation, so leave your android with Jules. Just in case, I suggest hiding some backup phone near the hospital.'

'Good point! Let's buy a couple along the road,' Henri agreed.

On the way to the hospital, Jiwon spoke on the phone in Korean. Henri, with his meager level of the language, could only pick out a couple of rather large numbers, from which he concluded that they were most likely talking about a mortgage for a house. Jules, without wasting extra minutes, as usual decided to fall asleep. This ability of his to "absorb time for sleep at any hour convenient for him" had fascinated Henri from childhood. *It's very practical*, he thought. *I wish I was like that.*

Opening his eyes, Henri found himself on Jules's shoulder. Unable to withstand the tight schedule of the last days, he had also learned to switch himself to "work-sleep" mode, just like a robot. Although…Intelligent robots would probably have dreams. Perhaps even several dreams at once. Dreams that span several human lives, of such as you or me.

'Leopold finally left us, I believe?' Jiwon asked him mockingly, holding out a bottle of cold coffee.

'He left you warm greetings and vowed to learn at least two new dances for the next meeting.' The young man wheezed, sipping coffee from the bottleneck.

'Why Langlais's older twin, after all? You don't have much time left, what do you want to know so badly?'

'I… It's just intuition for now,' he said uncertainly.

'Could you please clarify, in case we're taking you to the mental hospital? This is not a bed of roses,' she said, raising her left eyebrow skeptically.

'I suspect that Marie-Julie is still dead and the woman I saw at the appointment is her older twin brother, Charles, who underwent gender reassignment surgery. Perhaps only a partial operation. For example, he removed the Adam's apple and slightly corrected his face,' Henri explained, looking indifferently out the window.

'It's good that Jules isn't marrying her.' Jiwon snapped, nodding her head. 'Otherwise, it would be extremely inconvenient if he had to share a razor, sneakers, and a game console with his spouse.'

'What's the difference? Anyway, my sister-in-law will have clumsy hands like an octopus,' continued Henri.

'Predestination, just like… Like everywhere! Everywhere there is one continuous predetermination. By the way, I got a phone with a new SIM card while you were sleeping,' Jiwon said as she turned off the engine and parked at the curb, handing Henri a blue package. 'You need to choose a place nearby and hide it properly. Oh, there are also walkie-talkies, so let's check them at the same time.'

With a nod, Henri left the salon as quietly as possible closing the door behind him. After walking about fifteen meters from the car, he saw a suitable pile of stones under a tree and was about to start digging a small hole for his "treasures" as Jiwon got in touch by radio.

'Leopold… Leopold… Do you copy?' she asked in a low voice as she lounged in the driver's seat.

'Sounds like it's coming from the bottom of a well, Dr. Bak. It's even good, because there's a stereo effect,' the elder Lero answered, continuing to dig out the "capsule hotel" in which to hide his equipment.

'Kim called. He found something on those calls. It's too early to say yet, but most likely you're right. They were made from the same address,' she said switching to a whisper.

'So someone is taking us somewhere?'

'It's not clear yet,' she said confidently, half-turning and slightly hanging over the sleeping Jules. 'I don't know what's going on with this Trust, but I know that you'll get your Guppy out of this, I'm sure.'

Instead of answering, she heard only a series of interference. Even more surprising was that the radio was working properly again, as soon as it returned to its original position. Leaning over to Jules once more, she noticed with interest that the interference was repeated. Something here strongly influenced the radio waves from spreading.

'Interesting…' she whispered. 'Boy, are you made of ferrite?'

***

'Junior orderly Jeong Cheol needs to go to registration,' a familiar male voice was broadcasting into the intercom.

'Well…' Mademoiselle Cheol said to herself as quietly as possible, and immediately, involuntarily looked back. "I've been working here for almost three months and he won't remember that I'm a Nurse! The nurse! Moreover not the youngest one if we talk about experience, but who cares about the number of shifts and nights you spend in the hospital? Why, why Jeong Cheol are you carrying this burden?" The young nurse complained as she slowly descended the steps of the staff staircase in the north wing of the hospital. 'Eh!' Exhaling heavily, she pulled out a ginger-flavored energy bar from the left pocket of her uniform. 'Well, I don't seem to have much choice. Today you are my whole lunch,' Cheol drawled despondently as she unwrapped the bar and devoured it as she walked. 'How bitter,' she added, bored. 'And why do I always listen to others? I had to choose a bar with cherries or chocolate...or even just become a doctor. I shouldn't care what's more expensive, because I only have one bar a day.' She giggled. Miss Cheol suddenly stumbled and almost flew down the remaining five steps to the exit at the bottom of the staircase. Successfully hooking her shoulder against the door, she was able to stop the fall, escaping with only a small bruise on her left wrist.

'That's the payment I get for daydreaming,' she remarked sarcastically, putting the dropped pass back into her pocket. Rising to her feet the nurse first brushed herself off and then carefully smoothed the small folds on the form. 'Well... Where are you heading now?' she whispered touching the doorknob and breaking into a satisfied smile.

'Without slowing down, he raised his staff. And silently pointed to the sky,' Jeong Cheol Jeong quoted the famous poem and swinging the door open.

At the front desk, she saw a rather interesting scene. The director of the hospital himself gazed menacingly at the confused young clerk, desperately trying to find the coveted folder with the patient's personal file among the endless mountain of papers. Opposite them stood a Caucasian man who looked about thirty-five years old and a tall Korean woman in a black striped business suit. Judging by the manner of communication the girl must be his translator, Jeong Cheol observed to herself as she walked toward them.

'Good afternoon, dear guests! We are very glad to see you within the walls of our institution,' she began in impeccable English. 'You can call me Nurse Jeong Cheol. Let me accompany you to the recreation area while our colleague takes care of your documents.'

'Very kind of you, Mademoiselle Jeong Cheol,' said the European looking at her.

'Jeong Cheol, we'll finish here with Miss Hwang, and you can accompany Mr. Sartre to the ward. The second floor, room 205,' the director said sternly with a heavy Korean accent.

Nodding her head, Sister Cheol invited Henri to follow her to the southern part of the hospital. Following the nurse, he turned to look at the concentrating Jiwon one last time. He still couldn't get out of his head the situation with a bug or other source of radio interference somewhere on Jules's body. Taking a deep breath, he tried to put his thoughts in order without taking his eyes off his best friend. Catching his eye Dr. Bak distracted herself from her conversation with the hospital director, showing her thumb to Henri as he retreated down the hallway.

Finally focusing on his route, he noticed that the walls of the hospital were painted in a pleasant mint-turquoise color. Contrary to all Henri's expectations, there were a lot of people in the corridors. As Jiwon said, from 10 am to 2 pm the patients had visits to doctors according to the local schedule, where most of them were going now. After passing along a long corridor, they came to one of the stairs. Having risen to the second floor they almost immediately found themselves at the desired chamber.

The room that now belonged to Henri seemed to be very bearable and even luxurious for a hospital. Tall, Dutch-style ceilings, a long bookcase against the left wall, several photographs of a dog hanging on the wall… *Is that a pug?* he wondered to himself. Bed linen, paintings on the walls… In almost every detail of this room, here was an image of a flattened muzzle. *Hmmm… Dr. Bak still remembers how through my carelessness, I had the stupidity to compare her favorite breed of dogs with micropigs… Here's retribution,* he thought with a puzzled frown on his face.

'Something is wrong?' kindly asked the nurse, looking at the dumbfounded Henri's face as he stared at one of the portraits of the pug.

'Oh… This…' His face was twisted in something between disgust, misunderstanding, a fit of laughter, and confusion. 'My dog … Kimchi. He would have liked this room,' Henri said nervously with a smile.

'Sure. No one leaves this hospital dissatisfied,' the nurse mysteriously agreed, adding, 'Make yourself comfortable, Mr. Sartre. At 2 pm, there will be lunch for you, but for now, you can stay at here or go to the recreation room on the ground floor. After lunch, I'll take you on a guided tour.'

'Exciting,' he drawled, trying to be more authentic to the image of a lover of pugs and yoga.

'Make yourself at home,' added Miss Cheol closing the door behind her.

Henri put his bag on the bed and slowly turned to the window. This autumn had not yet had time to take life from the entire forest, so most of the trees were wearing summer green crowns. *Well…* he thought taking off his cufflinks and looking at the carefully ironed mint-blue robes for patients lying peacefully on a chair by the mirror, *it's Show Time.*

There was still about an hour to go before lunch, so after closing the door behind him and making sure that the key-pass to the room was working, Henri set off to wander the corridors. There were about twenty rooms on the second floor and judging by the nameplates, they all belonged to patients. The only exception was one office for the nurse on duty, and the utility room at the end of the corridor right at the entrance to the service staircase.

Judging by the inscriptions in Korean, which Henri, despite his "not advanced" level of language proficiency, still could understand, the entrance to the carer stairs was open only to hospital staff. Recalling a small detour on the way to the ward, he concluded that the only way to the fourth floor lay either through these service stairs or through the service elevator in the main building of the hospital.

Walking along past the rooms with the nameplates, past the empty rooms whose owners should now be attending doctors, Henri began to examine with curiosity the electronic lock on the door to the service staircase. In these circumstances, he had only two options. The first, not the most pleasant one, was to get a pass card from one of the staff, possibly with the use of sabotage. The second, a no less unpleasant plan consisted of sabotage by itself, but on a larger scale.

Hmm… Where should I start? he asked mentally, rubbing his chin until the maelstrom of his thoughts was interrupted by a sharp slap on the shoulder.

'Good afternoon, mister,' a rather gloomy man muttered in a raspy voice. Judging by his accent, he was not a native of this country. Analyzing his speech and particular manner of speaking, Henri concluded that he was most likely Japanese.

'Perhaps you are lost? I am Doctor Tsuru; let me take you to the restroom.' After finishing the sentence, the doctor smiled timidly, but for some reason only with the left half of his mouth. It looked very strange. 'Patients shouldn't wander the corridors during "visits to doctors" time,' he immediately added exposing the rest of the mouth, which was incredibly wide for such a small person, the right half of which was decorated with a rather massive incisor, which made the doctor's seemingly friendly smile look like the grin of a great white shark.

'Sorry…' It was about time to switch on the model of a "stupid white foreigner" in a way that had always worked for Henri in almost all Asian countries. 'I've only been here for a few hours and the hospital is so huge that

I couldn't figure out how to get down to the first floor. It looks like there's a staircase here,' he concluded, pointing to the service entrance signed in Korean.

'Oh, this is the service staircase. Only for staff,' the doctor said condescendingly, nodding toward Henri, patting him on the shoulder, and leading him toward the elevator in the west wing.

'How fortunate that you found me, Doctor Tsur,' Henri muttered with a smile, patting the doctor on the shoulder in response and at the same time trying to pull the pen out of the left pocket of his robe – as a warm-up before getting his pass card.

-'펜이 필요하세요? 내 주머니에서 다른 걸 찾길 바라십니까? (Do you need the pen that's in my pocket, or do you expect to find something else there, mister?)' Without turning his head the Japanese whispered in perfect Korean, and made a gesture, inviting Henri to the elevator.

'Did you say something to me, doctor?' asked Henri, and with a feigned raising of his eyebrows, slowly entered the cockpit.

'Oh, I was just trying to remember the lines from the five-line poetry of my favorite poet Yamabe no Akahito,' he replied pressing the button for the first floor.

'Off the beach at Waka

With the rising tide

The sandbanks vanish

Plunging to the reed beds…

Well, you must be aware of the sequel, but I just can't remember. Our esteemed director said that you are a literary critic, Mr. Sartre,' the doctor said smiling with the right side of his mouth, obviously deliberately exposing his right canine and looking tensely into the eyes of the man in front of him.

'Yes…' Henri said uncertainly leaving the elevator slowly. 'Of course, I know… I… I suppose I need to go left, there's a sign in English,' he added, nodding with one foot to the turn while still in the cockpit.

'The last line of the five-verse, Mr. Sartre,' the Japanese continued. 'Don't forget about that,' he finished, smiling as wide as possible as all thirty-two as if his teeth were now desperately trying to converge somewhere on the back of his head. In combination with wide-open and seemingly inhumanly large eyes in which a hostile flame was now burning, the doctor looked extremely creepy.

Squeezing out the remnants of friendliness and composure, like the last of the toothpaste from a tube already rolled into an iron bundle, Henri answered him with a half-smile and went to the rest room to take a breath.

Henri did not have to walk very far along the corridor. Just around the corner, he saw a rescue sign with the words "restroom." Even for such a large hospital, the premises were impressive, rather resembling an assembly hall. The center of the room was littered with plenty of soft mattresses and pastel-colored mini-gazebos. Different sections for patients were located around the perimeter of the room.

Several patients worked in the sculpting corner with semi-professional pottery wheels. In the art area with easels, a couple of people diligently drew a still life with a mentor. A little to the left, there was a ping-pong table fenced with a soundproof wall, where, despite being the time of visits to the doctors, several people had already gathered. The remaining seats along the right wall were occupied by tables with various board games: chess, Chinese go, dominoes, poker, perudo... In the left corner of the hall, there was a rather large aquarium.

'Excellent,' he said to himself. 'I need to sit down next to the aquarium to put my thoughts in order and calmly think about the plan of action.'

Slowly walking around the pavilions, he grabbed a soft pink pouffe and threw it down in front of the aquarium, and sat down to study its inhabitants. *So... Who do we have here? OU! What luck!* he thought. 'This is a white molly or a snowflake as Jules liked to call them in childhood. The individual was rather large, not less than ten centimeters, so definitely a female. Translucent fins of incredible beauty successfully combined with the silver color of its scales.'

Immediately behind the snowflake, Henri's eye caught a long-mouthed swordfish that strongly resembled a pike by its jaw. 'Strangely, they were settled nearby... Who do we have next? This is a golden mullet, or as some of Henri's friends call it, a "zhuravka," from the Ukrainian word meaning...a female crane? As far as he remembered, such a poetic name was connected with the fact that these fish living in the Black and Azov seas often jumped out of the water in fright, like a flock of cranes.'

'Do you like fish?' a voice spoke next to him in English.

Having been dragged away from his thoughts by a question from the outside, he saw two dark gray eyes looking at him closely through the aquarium. Tilting his head behind the aquarium, he considered his interlocutor. It was a red-haired woman who looked about 30–35 years old. Mademoiselle's hair was not styled properly for a secular exit, and stuck out in disarray in all directions. The length of her hair saved the day, giving it them to still obey the laws of gravity.

Despite her frightening hairstyle, Henri noted that mademoiselle was very pretty and well-built. In general, she was a bit thin for his taste, but the main detail that he always paid attention to in women could not fail to delight him – her wrists were simply amazing. She was holding an impressive notebook tablet at her right breast and with her left hand was making some sketches in it, apparently drawing fish. Her eyes tried to catch the movement of the inhabitants of the aquarium, which caused her eyebrows to be pulled together, which generally gave her face a rather stern expression.

'Not all, miss, not all. There are different fish.' Henri held out, and unexpectedly for him, smiled charmingly.

'I think they are also not happy with you,' the stranger said indifferently without taking her eyes off her occupation.

'Can I clarify how the lady came to this conclusion?' intrigued Henri asked, simply glowing with curiosity.

'There's a huge amount of fish droppings on your half of the aquarium. As soon as they see you, they all do it at once,' she explained sternly, removing the red hair from her face.

'Well, maybe it happens to them from excitement when they meet with something beautiful?' Henri retorted, still not taking his eyes off the girl.

A minute later his interlocutor for the first time during their dialogue tore her eyes from the notebook and looked directly at Henri. With a searching glance, she ran first over his face, then quickly scanned his torso and arms, finally fixing her gaze on his fingers. After about thirty seconds, she moved her chair in his direction and gave an expressive look, in Henri's eyes, and answered.

'No, it's unlikely. You are very ugly.' Having finished with the phrase on duty, as if the conversation was about flowers or the weather, the red-haired immediately returned to her drawing.

Monsieur Leroy was initially taken aback by her words, but five seconds later, he was laughing eagerly at her answer. At first, she did not respond at all to such a reaction, but after a minute, she added, 'And on top of that, he's very stupid.'

Henri could not stand the second round, and immediately bent away from laughter, so amusing did these words sound coming from a hyper serious girl in a hospital robe with some semblance of a bird's nest on her head, diligently drawing aquarium fish in the patient's rest room.

Are you also French? You have a French accent, Henri wondered, but the girl didn't answer him. 'You know,' he continued, 'it's interesting that before settling into his house of actinia' – he nodded at the fish floating next to the clownfish – 'these amazing fishes allow themselves to be stung, neatly. In response to this irritation their body produces protective mucus.' Having finished speaking, he waited with interest for a reaction, but again there was no answer.

'My name is Emmanuel. And what is your name?' Without losing the attempts to establish at least some kind of contact, he continued, 'You know, I arrived just a few hours ago and I still don't quite understand how everything works here,' he explained, but the girl, as if not hearing his words, continued to draw persistently.

'Do you know anything about what there is on the fourth floor?' Henri asked her in a whisper, in principle, not even hoping for any answer, but the girl suddenly stopped and without changing her position, silently moved her chair closer to him.

'Anyone who comes at midnight always knows where he should have been, even if he is not there. They're all looking for him,' she said mysteriously. 'And you... Is someone looking for you?' With a jerk bending over the dumbfounded Henri, she stopped just a couple of centimeters from his nose. 'They are already looking,' she continued, 'or have they already found him?'

She jerked abruptly and looking at her watch, got up from her chair and threw her notebook on the floor. Turning unhurriedly, she walked toward the exit, along with a good portion of the room's visitors. Slowly shifting his gaze from the leaving girl to the clock, Henri was surprised to note that it was lunchtime. Five minutes to two, Seoul time.

Well, he thought, *it's unlikely that I will be able to learn from the locals something worthwhile, plus I haven't had time to get hungry yet. So while the bulk of the patients will be in the canteen, it's better to rest near the offices, perhaps somewhere I will find some pass. Besides, I need to understand where they have a transformer or local power shield for a diversion.* Confidently getting up from the pouffe, Henri was about to walk toward the exit, but suddenly stopped at the very entrance. He had a very strong feeling that he had forgotten something.

Returning to the aquarium, he realized that he had been carrying nothing with him, except for the pass to his room. The phantom sensation of a mobile phone in his hand still haunted him. 'The gadgets have penetrated too deeply into our hearts,' Henri remarked with a grin, turning around, but immediately realized that he was wrong. The reason he had returned was now lying on the floor in front of him. From the pages of the same notebook-tablet thrown down by the red-haired woman, a Japanese crane, painted in great detailcrane, was looking up at him. 'But…' he whispered, 'didn't she sketch the fish?' Slowly lifting the notebook from the floor, he straightened the collar of his shirt, smoothed his hair, and walked toward the exit and the dining room. 'What did Jiwon say about the messenger? Follow the white crane?'

Walking down the corridor, Henri easily found the dining room. There were an especially large number of visitors at this hour, but even though they were not quite ordinary people, there was no sense of fuss. Quite the opposite, there was a rather suspicious silence in the room, where at the moment there were about fifty people. Looking around the hall, he immediately found a table at which his "white crane" was already drinking tea in very interesting company. To her left sat an old man who was unfamiliar to him, a man with bulging "telescope goldfish" eyes and directly opposite him was a young patient who, leaning her elbows on the table, was fast asleep. Deftly going around two adjacent tables, Henri caught the eye of Mademoiselle Crane, nodding politely to which she nodded back to him, so he quickly landing in one of the empty chairs.

'It wasn't very civil of you to sit down without being invited.' His red-haired acquaintance immediately hissed in a hoarse voice.

'Yes, but you nodded to me and I thought…' Henri was taken aback; he did see her nod in return.

'I never nodded to you. I rarely nod at all,' she replied with a reproachful look.

'It is common for nodders to see nods everywhere. Nodding, they get a slight degree of concussion.' The man suddenly entered into the dialogue, continuously stroking his left hand, like a beloved pet.

'I don't dare to bother you,' Henri said, smiling as broadly as possible, getting up from the table.

'Teatime,' the redhead shouted, placing a teacup next to him with a crash.

'With sugar?' sitting down back in his place, Henri agreed.

'Honey without bees from India, as Onesikrit wrote,' the elderly man drawled thoughtfully.

'One dollar a teaspoon was given by the British at the beginning of the fourteenth century,' the redhead added, stirring her tea.

'The Caribbean islands are a granary of sugar,' the sleeping girl suddenly whispered, outwardly remaining motionless.

Interesting, Henri thought, *they seem to have one mind for three. How chaotic they are in conversation. Well... Let's try to walk by your rules.*

- Horses galloped somewhere,
Slender like a willow,
Light as a breath of freedom,
Fast as a time of idling,
Glorious as the sun.

If these gorgeous horses,
Could be someone's thoughts.
Thoughts that thought their vertex,
Flying out with banging,
Fell to the ground.

Maybe somewhere maybe,
Jumping through the branches.
Those that I am undeniable,
I Will call as my own.

Thought is not for choosing.
Horse-shape or like a monkey.
The main thing matters,
Whether they get shot.

Having finished reading, Henri waited for the reaction of his companions. The man seemed to like this creation, judging by the fact that he slightly raised the visor of an imaginary hat and nodding in his direction. The red-haired woman, without saying anything, just silently pushed her chair a little further away from Henri. The sleeping person quietly slapped her hand on the table, which could well be taken for some semblance of applause. Had he finally found his audience?

'I have a friend here. He is also French and also writes poetry. Wonderful poems, much better than this one. However, the trouble is that I cannot find him. I think his room is somewhere on the fourth floor,' Henri said as he began sipping from his cup.

'Hey!' The "sleeping girl," raising her head, suddenly entered the conversation. 'We seem to have a schizophrenic here with an imaginary friend. There are no patient rooms on the fourth floor.'

'Only if he's not talking about a ghost,' the redhead retorted without looking up from her cup.

'A ghost?' Henri asked with interest, raising his eyebrows.

'Room 402,' the man explained. 'The only unknown room on the fourth floor. The nurses once whispered that they were carrying food there in shifts, but who was there and what was inside they did not know. Food is delivered only to a special table at the door to the ward without going inside. Only the director of the hospital can go there personally, so no one has ever been there and cannot say with certainty if someone is there, or not. Perhaps it's just the director's private quarters.'

'Cracker time,' the nurse announced, handing out two round biscuits to the dining patients.

Henri was about to start eating the treatment he received, but immediately got a slap on his hand from the redhead. Leaning closer to him, she silently took his head with her hands and turned it to the right. The picture before his eyes was one of the strangest he had ever seen. Without saying a word, like ants, all the patients without exception lined up in a long queue in front of the table, laying out their offerings before a frightening bald guy with a disproportionately large head above his body. The man greedily shoved the cookies into his mouth with the back of his hand while mooing terribly. After giving the cookies, the patients left the dining room, which meant the end of the mealtime.

Without further ado, Henri followed suit, mechanically placing the contents of his hand on the big-head's table.

'At 9 p.m. in the restroom near the aquarium. During the Hobby club 'performance,' Mademoiselle Crane quietly whispered before leaving the dining room. 'Just put on something less gaudy,' she concluded, casting an appraising glance at his robe. He would certainly have taken her words into account if it hadn't been for the fact that he was now wearing the standard uniform worn by all the patients in this hospital, including herself.

'I will try to choose something to match your outfit,' Henri whispered with a smile, noting that apparently his stay here would certainly not be boring.

He had to catch up with the missed morning round of doctor's consultations during a quiet afternoon, having finished just in time for dinner and taking medications. The initial appointments of specialists, accompanied by the charming nurse Jeol, were satisfied with the routine. Everyone copied the information already indicated in his file and carried out an external examination. All this of course was very tedious, but on the whole, it was not at all difficult for him to weave a web of legends about himself as Emmanuel Sartre.

The last for today was the final appointment with one of the hospital's psychiatrists, a Dr. Hwang Jisok. Anticipating a series of questions regarding his pseudo-depression, he mentally went over the possible versions lying on a comfortable leather couch. Dr. Hwang, who strongly resembled a sea stingray in his dexterous speech pirouettes, slowly wrote down the missing information on his card.

'So, Monsieur Sartre, I would like to begin our conversation with your condition today. Please describe to me how you feel at the moment.'

'Hmm…' Henri hesitated, recalling the traits of lingering depression he read this morning. 'I feel a little anxious about my family and career. It saddens me to realize that my favorite activities no longer bring me the pleasure that they used to do. I don't sleep well and I often get headaches,' he finished, dramatically placing his hand on his left temple.

'That's how…' The doctor wrote down, shaking his head. 'And what about your appetite?'

'I have lost a lot of weight over the past year, about almost four kilograms. Maybe for some people that might seem insignificant, but I'm already a rather skinny guy, so four kilograms is quite a bit for me,' Henri continued, putting his hands on his stomach.

'Four kilograms…' The doctor wrote down with satisfaction. 'Eating disorder, apathy… Tell me, please, about your relationship with your ex-wife. I read that it was a pretty painful break up and she's still mad at you. This is true?'

'I…' Henri desperately tried to present a picture of a fictional ex-wife to one of his past passions, but none of them could play this role, even if only imaginatively. Throughout the thirty-three years of his life, he preferred to keep to his own comforts, and to his surprise, he realized that he had never even cohabited with any of his passions. The relationship was that he even had a separate closet in his apartment for his girlfriends, but all the romance began and ended with the weekend. Sometimes he could allow his girlfriend to show up in the middle of the week if the work schedule allowed it.

In principle, all his darlings were prudent and independent ladies, perfectly understanding about the format of relations they subscribe to, and therefore, in front of any of them, he was not particularly ashamed of his actions. All adults and everyone understood that if something went wrong, then everyone was free to return to their corner. However, despite the rather rigid framework in communication, his emotional coldness, and rather an ordinary appearance, a considerable number of representatives of the opposite sex always hovered around Henri, even in childhood.

Childhood… And then Henri's heart slowed down. *Well*, he thought. *I just had time to lie down on the couch in the psychologist's office when paranoia began.* He knew that a worm named Marie-Julie would soon wake up again.

'If you're uncomfortable talking about it, Emmanuel, then try to describe to me one of your dialogues or an evening spent with your spouse. This will help us understand the feelings and emotions you experienced,' Dr. Hwang continued while correcting his glasses.

'I will try my best…' Squeezed Henri with a smile in an attempt to tune in to the right way of proceeding.

So, Henri mentally tuned in. 'Try to remember one of the evenings with Marie-Julie, plunge into your memories. Leisurely I pull off my robe, discard my slates because all the surplus must remain on the floor. Mentally preparing myself for immersion in the cold waters of the aquarium made from my memories. I slow my breath, trying to delay the look at one point. Four… I never loved her. Three…everything that was between us meant nothing to me. Two… I would never remember her if it wasn't for that reception meeting. One… Marie-Julie…'

'It's cold…' began Henri. 'I will never get even a degree warmer. Every cell of mine trembles, hoping to keep warm in some way. My veins still try to bring to my heart at least a drop of heat. The Sunday sun gives the first rays to this musty earth. The flower on the table became another three millimeters closer to the south. It is so natural for everything alive – to reach for the light.'

'Are you sleeping?' she asked, lying at the head of the bed, throwing her left hand over her head. A shock of her dark and heavy-as-steel cable hair spilled over the bed, revealing a thin coffee-colored neck. Then, under the sun, she looked like a roasted coffee bean. Her nose twitched with displeasure giving out her discomfort. For sure, she then lay down her left hand. This is very impractical for a left-hander; however, whatever she did was impractical. She never worried if I could understand her since this was perhaps the only person on earth who did not care about the fact that most of our communication did not understand me. 'If we hurry, we will still have time,' she whispered, stroking her chin.

'I'm asleep,' I replied once again looking at the clock.

'Where did your wife want to invite you? Where did you miss?' the fascinated doctor asked, taking off his glasses.

'I… I think I didn't care so much that I don't remember. Doctor, am I a terrible person?' Henri said desperately.

'You are a human being, and while your march through this wonderful world continues, you have time to grow,' the doctor concluded with a joke, closing his notebook in which he had been making notes. 'Let's finish for today. You need to be in time for dinner before the show starts. As part of our art therapy, we conduct various seminars and master classes. Today we are putting on an excerpt from the opera, "Havoc in heaven" based on Wu Cheng'en's "Journey to the West."

With a grateful nod, Henri cautiously got up from the couch and, saying goodbye to the doctor, hurried to the concert hall. Along the way, he grabbed a couple of sandwiches from the dining room. He leisurely walked around the first floor of the building in search of an electrical control room. As far as his level of Korean made it clear to him, it was located in the main building. The entrance to the room was guarded by a combination lock, which somewhat facilitated the issue with a pass. It only remained to cause a small short circuit so that the right employee showed up there to make a check.

There weren't many video cameras on the ground floor, plus a men's restroom was located nearby. The idea was quite simple. Henri just had to take the light bulb out, short-circuit its base, put it back, and turn on the light again. Voilà, and with a slight movement of the hand, the entire first floor was de-energized.

Coming out of the men's room, Henri went to the cooler and poured himself a glass of water, then walked confidently toward the switchboard, and settled down around the corner so that he could see the combination lock from afar. The appearance of an electrician did not take long – only ten minutes, and they were there. 1932020…seven cherished numbers separating it from the entrance. Ten minutes… He will only have ten minutes when the doors would be unlocked to get from the first to the fourth floor through the service stairs, and talk to Charles.

'Monsieur Sartre?' Henri's reflections were interrupted by a creaky male voice that belonged to the director of the hospital. 'Well, how was your first day? Have you already made friends with someone?'

'So far only with a couple of people, sir, but I promise to fix these indicators soon.' Getting up he held out his palm for a handshake.

The director smiled slightly and hesitated a little while shaking his hand.

'Have we met you before, Mr. Sartre? You have very familiar eyes.'

'Yes, we saw each other this morning,' Henri answered discouragingly.

'Have we met before this morning?' his inquisitor insisted.

'Mr. Director,' a nurse in a beautiful pale pink robe interrupted their conversation, 'the power outage has been eliminated. Our event starts as scheduled in ten minutes.'

'Perfect. Mister Sartre, let's go into the hall,' the director finished patting him on the shoulder and pointing straight down the corridor. Henri smiled and followed him. Even though everything was going well enough, he entered the room with a sense of foreboding.

A huge number of guests gathered in the hospital's assembly hall. Not only the hospital staff and patients but also their relatives were invited to the performance.

'It's such a shame that you didn't see the first show. We made it in the form of a theatrical performance based on "Journey to the West." This time, we decided to continue creating in this direction, but we took the risk of going for an experiment, and this time we are showing the backstory about the Monkey King in an operatic format,' the director of the hospital told him while drinking orange juice and showing him the hall.

'I hope in the format of the Peking Opera?' Henri asked drinking from a plastic glass of water.

'Yes, that's why I was asked to open the concert with a short introduction briefly describing the events shown. Are you familiar with the story of the Monkey King, Monsieur Sartre?'

'Good enough. I have a long history with him,' Henri said with a smile.

'The beginning is intriguing. Can you explain?' asked the director interested.

'I was once very repulsed by this character. The fact is that I took his stubbornness for pride and stubbornness until the "curse of the Monkey King" fell on me.'

'Curse of the Monkey King?' the director asked ironically.

'Yes. All the food with his image that I ate or just used, gave me indigestion or allergies. At that time, I often visited China and crossed paths with it in many places. This continued until reviewing one of the adaptations for this novel when I finally realized that the qualities that angered me so much in him are those qualities from which I suffer. They are stubbornness and pride. These qualities did not belong to the Monkey King; they belonged to me. The qualities he had are an unshakable will and persistence. This is how I see him now, this is how I want to become now. After all, I believe that only unshakable will and persistence can change this world. As soon as I realized this, the curse ceased to exist for me,' clutching an empty glass, Henri finished his story.

'Curious,' the director began, but he was immediately interrupted by a nurse who approached him.

'Mr. Director, we're starting. We ask you to take a seat in the front row.'

Henri silently nodded to the nurse and walked to the place he'd previously noted at the end of the hall, so that he could imperceptibly leave to meet with Mademoiselle Crane.

'Good evening, dear friends,' the host of the evening, and founder and leader of the local drama club, greeted all those present with almost no accent. 'My name is Dr. Bong Joon-ho. Let me congratulate everyone on the fact that today we are ready to present to you our second production based on the legendary work of Wu Cheng'en's "Journey to the West."'" The audience warmly greeted the presenter's words with applause. The first concert was very successful. Today's performance will be held in the format of a classical Chinese Peking Opera, and in order not to get everybody confused with the plot of the work, we asked our dear director, Moon Zhehe, to open the concert with an introductory speech highlighting the plot of our show.'

The hall cordially greeted the director and he ascended the stage and slowly began his speech.

'A long time ago, on Mount Huago, near the city of Luoyang, not far from Zhengzhou, which we all know, there was a magic stone. Having absorbed the forces of heaven and earth, it gave birth to a stone monkey. The fearless monkey became king over all the inhabitants of that mountain, but this was not enough for him. To gain more strength and break the endless cycle of reincarnation, to protect his folk forever, he became a disciple of a sage famous in ancient times. The sage gave the monkey the Buddhist name of Sun Wukong, which is translated from Chinese as "who cognized emptiness." After a long period of training, Sun Wukong mastered the secrets of the five elements and seventy-two transformations. He got golden hoops in the palace of the Dragon King and stole equipment from the four Dragon Kings. Once he even managed to erase his name from the book of "Life and Death." The heavenly gods were afraid of Sun Wukong and even invited him to heaven for appeasing, but devoted to his folk he stayed with them and rebelled against the gods, calling himself a great sage, equal to them. So Sun Wukong unleashed the Great War in which even the most powerful gods could not cope with the angry Monkey King. However, even though no one could defeat Sun Wukong' – here the director paused – 'to the Great Buddha he was just an ordinary monkey. Defeated by him, Sun Wukong spent five hundred years imprisoned in cold crystal in the Mountain of Five Elements, from where the story of the previous show began. As you can see, the persistence and unshakable will of the Monkey King, although it could influence the course of events, did not change the universe in any way. Laws and social structure are unshakable and eternal things.' The director finished to applause, and then took his place in the front row.

'Laws and social norms?' Henri whispered looking at the stage where the actors had already appeared. 'And I naively believed that only love and evolution can be unshakable and eternal.'

Turning his head to the guests sitting next to him, he saw an obvious interest on the part of the public in everything that was happening. Sure, such stories of falls after dizzy heights have always been the most desirable dish for the crowd who loves to amuse itself.

Henri turned his gaze to the clock near the entrance to the hall, which showed fifteen minutes to nine in the evening. Judging by the dance of the battle with the dragon king the performance would take at least another hour. Trying not to attract attention to himself, Henri walked as quietly as possible to the table with the drinks and, pouring himself a tomato juice, then tiptoed out into the corridor.

The way to the restroom from the assembly hall took about six minutes. From there, it takes two minutes to reach the switchboard, plus three minutes to climb the stairs from the first to the fourth floor. In principle, he had enough time. Going over in his head various ways to start a conversation with Charles Langlaist, Henri didn't notice how he got to the meeting place. There was no light in the break room, only moonlight shining through the plastic blinds. Mademoiselle Crane swayed slowly in her chair as if it were a rocking chair, as she admired the moon. Her face, usually filled with contempt or concern, was finally relaxed and did not express any emotion.

'Beautiful night,' she said suddenly.

Henri carefully moved one of the chairs closer to the lady and without saying too much, just sat down next to her, admiring her full month.

'You're not one of them, are you?' she blurted out suddenly, ceasing to sway, still looking out the window.

'And you?' without turning his head, he asked in response.

The redhead said nothing, just continued to sway in her chair.

'Can you help me in the electrical room? I want to ask you to pull the switch, then I will have time to run up the staff stairway to the fourth floor. The conversation will take about ten minutes, after which we will meet at the emergency exit in the kitchen. By the way, how do we get through the guards at the gate?'

'Let's go through like moonlight,' she whispered, getting up from her chair and heading for the exit.

'As always, in great detail,' Henri whispered with a slight smile. 'What a pity that Jules has already chosen a bride.'

Catching up with his companion, he noted that from the backside and in this semi-darkness and with her slightly swaying gait, she looked like a pirate.

'Did you fall asleep there?' burst out the red-haired lightly patting him on the shoulder.

Henri immediately felt a sharp cutting pain burning through his left arm and gradually spreading throughout his body. Looking from the hospital floor to the source of the pain, he saw her holding his left hand which was drooping unnaturally like a rag. Too unnatural... As if... 'The hand didn't come out of the joint, did it?' Henri panicked, perplexedly going over all possible options in his head.

'You'd better go straight to the staff stairs; let's not waste too much time. Just tell me the code from the control room,' Mademoiselle Crane whispered, scratching her chin.

'W... Good,' he said slowly, feeling the pain gradually recede and noticing that his left arm was fine again. '1932020,' said Henri and walked on padded feet to the service staircase.

The strange sensation in his left hand still did not leave him, although the previous pain was gone.

'So, another ten meters to the right, then a turn to the left, two meters straight...' he said mentally. 'And here is the staircase! Well, another minute and...' A sudden attack of pain was so strong that he fell to the ground and began to choke. Convulsively trying to regain his breathing, he nervously beat himself in the chest, going over all the possible options for the cause of what was happening in his head.' Was there poison in the tomato juice or the sandwich? Perhaps something was sprayed in the air, or is it still the unfortunate aneurysm that's transmitted to many men in his family, but for some reason had bypassed him in his youth. Could it be the return of the Monkey King's curse? I left the middle of the concert!' From the last thought to a strong attack of coughing, an uncontrolled burst of laughter was added.

'*I can't even die like a normal person.*' Flashed through his head. 'By the way, maybe this is the curse of the Trust? Then it's good that it's me and not Jules,' Henri whispered just as the light in the entire wing immediately went out. 'Time has passed... I have only ten minutes.'

Forcing himself to stand up, he immediately rushed to the stairs. As intended, all the locks were unbolted, so that the main factor that would play against him now was time. Getting to the third floor Henri felt a severe shortness of breath; the recent seizure didn't plan to let him go so soon. Having given himself a rest for about ten seconds, he strained to overcome the last frontier and was near the entrance to the cherished fourth floor.

To his surprise, there was no emergency lighting as such. Only a few rather dim warning signs of a dark-burgundy hue were blinking, which made the entire surrounding environment reminiscent to Henri of footage from an old horror film. Before him was a dark empty corridor whose deathly silence was broken only by the sound of his breathing. So, room 402... Only a couple of seconds separated Henri from a conversation with a person who, if possible, he would prefer not to meet again. Exhaling nervously, he confidently walked forward...

'Calm down. He gave no reasons to blame me for anything. Marie-Julie is alive and all the negativity that he had in my address was just a stupid childhood grievance, so...' Henri's line of thought was interrupted by an extraneous sound.

Suddenly, one of the doors at the end of the dark corridor opened, making him stand still in fright. The creak of the door pierced the silence immediately drowning in it, and again leaving Henri alone with his own treacherously loud heartbeat.

'Calm down... It's just a door,' he mentally persuaded himself. *'Let's look...'* The silence was again broken by an extraneous sound, but this time they were steps, or rather, three steps. Three steps, after which a dark silhouette slowly approaching him appeared next to the open door.

Henri stood on the opposite side of the burning sign, so if he could hold back the oncoming cough he would remain unnoticed by this stranger. All that remained was to wait until the extraneous silhouette matched the burning sign so that it could be seen. Holding his breath, Henri waited. He waited while the stranger walked slowly in his direction, most likely intending to leave the floor. Step, second, third... The silhouette suddenly froze before reaching the sign, remaining in the blind zone.

'Why you are not in your chamber?' the stranger addressed him in English.

'나는 전기입니다. 조명 확인(I'm an electrician. I'm checking the lighting),' he replied sure that his face was impossible to make out in such darkness.

'Henri?' He was thunderstruck by the words that came from the void. 'Henri Lero, is that you?' The stranger came out on the dark burgundy light of the emergency pointer to show his face. In front of him was a man whom he had last seen alive almost nineteen years ago. A face he remembered still quite young, but knew too well not to recognize. It was the face of a young man whose photograph he had seen in the second January issue of the French economic magazine "Challenges" earlier this year. Before him stood none other than his former classmate, Oberon Bernard, who officially died in the fire along with his entire family three months ago.

***

'Hurry up, we haven't much time,' complained the eldest of the Lero children, nervously scrolling in his hand the morning cookies hidden in his pocket. When exactly he did this, Henri did not remember, but without giving the cookies to the local bigheaded feudal lord, by local standards, he probably committed a real tax crime and therefore it was completely undesirable to stay in this place. It was even more undesirable to linger in the storage of the patients' personal belongings, where the guards could appear any minute.

'Wait for a second, I'll just put on my sneakers. Is it cold outside? They haven't let me out of the fourth floor for a hundred years,' complained Oberon, meticulously sorting through the clothes in the bags.

'But it successfully helped you avoid concerts of local amateur performances. Right now, by the way, there is one. Throw on a sweater or sweatshirt and please donate one to me too.'

Oberon put his hand into one of the bags and pulled out the first sweatshirt he came across and threw it to Henri.

'Well, I'm ready. What's our plan?'

'Down the stairs and into the kitchen to the emergency exit, where my messenger is waiting for us. She will lead us through the security at the gate,' Henri answered leaving the vault.

'She? Oh… Monsieur Lero!' lighting up the darkness of the corridor with a snow-white smile, Oberon said with satisfaction. 'Years go by, but you are still the same indomitable womanizer, as you were during your studies at boarding school. I never seemed to have the slightest chance of getting your attention.'

'Years go by, but I still hear the same non-intellectual jokes,' Henri retorted calmly. By the way, unlike some others, I grew up so that I switched from the number of relationships to quality.'

'Okay, but I hardly believe it.'

'By the way, why don't you ask why I'm here?' Henri wondered, raising his eyebrows inquiringly.

'What for? You must have a white horse with you because you're saving me from the tower with a dragon, my lovely prince,' Oberon replied, slapping Henri on the shoulder. This was a big man's hand, by the way, and very heavy.

'I will not develop this topic, because your jokes in this direction, just like many years ago, still seem rather strange to me.'

'Come on. I was joking, I'm joking, and I will joke this way only with you.'

'It also worries me. By the way, you could invite me to the movies at least once. Of course, I would not agree, but that would clarify everything.'

'I have no idea what you're talking about.'

'Okay. It's your business, but if you stubbornly do not want to notice something, this does not mean that it does not exist. Even if you don't, someone else will see it.'

'So, I will make them see everything the way I need it,' stated the ultimatum Oberon, contentedly raising his palms as always.

Henri mentally pitied the guy, but actively suppressed his feelings. No, it's not bad to be confident in your convictions, but how poor is the world of those who, despite absolutely everything that surrounds him, sees only two colors, stubbornly denying that there is a whole rainbow to be seen.

The emergency lighting in the kitchen was rather dim, but had a rather pleasant purple-blue hue, giving the room the impression that the room was underwater.

'Are you sure they'll be waiting for us here?' Oberon expressed his doubt as he leaned on the doorframe.

'I'll take a look in the back room.' Henri slid along the left wall, but before he'd even taken two steps he froze, on hearing another extraneous sound.

'Why didn't you go back to your chamber, mister? I don't remember your face…' Henri was afraid to turn around, in case he gave himself away. One of the doctors had found Oberon. We can only hope that he will figure out how to pretend to be one of the relatives of the patients who came to today's concert.

Fortunately, sweaters worn over a hospital robe could well confuse the doctor. The stranger's voice was very, very familiar.

'I came to support my sister; she performed today,' Oberon answered rather confidently, not sounding at all bewildered.

'Oh, yes, the concert,' the doctor drawled thoughtfully, with an interesting accent either in German or... Stop. It was a Japanese accent. Japanese! Henri swallowed nervously. Behind him stood that creepy Japanese doctor.

'Did you like the concert, mister?' the Japanese doctor continued, with curiosity.

Well, thought Henri, *the main thing now is that he does not get confused and does not blurt out his name in a state of shock. Come on, Oberon, pull yourself together! You will succeed.*

'Lero... Mister Lero,' Oberon said at the same moment.

Is he serious? He really couldn't think of any other French surname? mentally switching to a cry, Henri wondered. 'Come on, you might as well also call yourself Henri to fully declassify me.'

'An-an-n-n-Andre...' said Oberon, apparently completely losing the remnants of his mind in this hospital.

'Brilliant,' Henri said to himself, rolling his eyes. 'This must be the pinnacle of the art of conspiracy. Conspiracy in its purest form.'

'André Lero?' asked the Japanese.

'Yes, it sounds very funny, doesn't it? My parents are real jokers,' continued Oberon, making the situation even worse. 'Although I am grateful to them that they didn't call me some girlish name. Like Henri, for example.'

'The name Henri, as far as I remember, is the equivalent of the German Heinrich? It seems to mean "head of the house" or "master,"' the doctor drawled contentedly. 'I like to delve into the etymology of names and surnames. For example, my surname translates as...' The phrase was completed by a sharp slap and a frightened cry from Oberon.

Turning around, Henri saw Dr. Tsuru lying on the floor unconscious. Mademoiselle Crane stood over him with a wooden stool in her hands. Oberon stood nearby, looking alternately at Henri and the redhead.

'Where have you been?' Their companion snorted in displeasure, throwing the stool aside and going to the refrigerator.

'My friend is a quarter English,' Henri began, bending over the doctor lying on the floor and checking his pulse. Fortunately, the doctor's pulse and breathing were normal. The wounds on his head were also not visible; therefore, he would wake up pretty quickly and get off with just a small bump. 'As you know, the British do not leave without a cup of tea and at least one game of bridge.' Having finished, he looked at the clock hanging over the door. They had less than a minute.

'Follow me.' Pulling a bottle out of the refrigerator, Mademoiselle Crane pushed the emergency door. Henri nodded to Oberon and they followed her.

The door opened onto the backyard of the hospital, next to a small garden. There was no security on this site, but it was also impossible to get out through this area. Although the barbed wire on top of the fence should now be without tension, the fence itself was too high to jump over it – about two and a half meters in height.

'What is she doing?' Oberon asked, pushing him aside.

Henri looked up to see the red-haired woman actively tinkering with the lawnmower.

'No... She's not going to...' he whispered, not believing what was happening.

Turning to them the redhead pulled out from behind her a strange object, covered with an old gardening glove. Having done no less strange manipulations, she first tilted it and then put it back.

'Henri... Please calm me down. Tell me this lawnmower is not gasoline, because from the smell...' Oberon began coughing.

'Okay. It doesn't smell like gasoline. The bottle she had taken from the kitchen was not a glass bottle of olive oil. She had no matches in her pocket and she won't burn the hospital down with a Molotov cocktail.' Henri rapped out without blinking.

At this time, their companion slowly pulled out a lighter from her pocket and set fire to the glove stuck in the bottle, then went around the corner and threw the bottle over the fence in the direction of the main entrance. Judging by the sound of the buzzing alarm, she had just hit one of the cars parked at the gate of the building.

'Well, let's go? Or do you want to have another game of poker?' The cold-blooded red-head turned her head to look at the puzzled guy.

'Yes... Come on. By the way, bridge, not...' Henri wanted to correct her joke, but after catching her creepy look, he immediately added, 'Bridge is not a very interesting game compared to poker.'

Mademoiselle Crane said nothing but continued to step toward the main gate, which at this time was deserted. All the security had now gone to attend to the mini-fire.

'Almost snatched her from you just now, Mr. Hero Lover,' whispered Oberon, hitting Henri on the shoulder with his fist.

'Oh, thank you. I appreciate your support, Mr. André Léro.' Henri parried.

'And what? It's a popular French surname.'

'Really? Do you know even one more Lero, except me?'

'Sure. I know Jules.' Smirked Oberon. 'Hey!' he added on seeing their companion already running out of the gate.

Increasing speed, they followed her example. The crowd on the street was small, with about five guards and three doctors. Carefully ducking along the wall, they hid behind cars standing on the opposite side of the gate from the burning car, where the red-haired woman was waiting for them.

'Let's crawl under the cars along the perimeter and then into the forest,' she whispered.

Looking at the tall Oberon, Henri was skeptical about the idea. Although if you looked closely, the guy has lost quite a lot of weight since their last meeting, so in theory, he should be able to crawl through. They'd have to go around the hospital from the other side to go toward the cache with the telephone and walkie-talkies, but these were trifles.

'Can you get through?' Henri nodded toward Oberon.

'Oh, you have no idea how deep the rabbit hole goes,' Oberon replied with a shrug, crawling under the brand new Fiat standing in front of him. The redhead followed him in silence. Henri exhaled deeply and looked anxiously at the still-burning car.

'Curiouser and curiouser,' he whispered and the next moment, he dived under the car.

Chapter 5
Sea Angel

'Faster! I can hear the dogs.' Mademoiselle Crane threw over her shoulder, moving suspiciously quickly through the forest in her hospital slippers.

'Dogs? But I don't... Henri, we've been running for more than half an hour, let's take a break? I have no strength.' Oberon gasped, stopping and greedily gasping for air.

'You've grown old, buddy. I remember that at school you were a marathon runner, but here we haven't even covered ten kilometers,' Henri quipped coming closer.

'You'd be like this, too, after three months trapped within the four walls of a hospital,' Oberon answered with a charming smile. 'By the way, Henri, why did the parents ask you to release me?'

Oh no... Henri thought and his heart ached for his friend. *He knows nothing at all about the fire, nothing about what happened to his family?* Noticing the confused look on Henri's face, Oberon immediately corrected himself.

'Oh, don't think anything bad. You have no idea how glad I am to see you, but...you understand,' he finished, smiling, as he once again hit Henri on the shoulder.

'I...' Raindrops running through the hood of the sweatshirt flowed down to his hair and face. Henri felt a lump rise to his throat. He just couldn't tell him that, not now. 'We need to catch up with her,' he blurted out and trudged after the redhead. 'It's about two more kilometers to the cache with the phones.'

He ran forward as fast as he could, feeling the raindrops on his face mingling with tears.

'So where is she from? Police? Intelligence service?' asked Oberon nodding toward Mademoiselle Crane who was by now about fifty meters ahead of them.

'Geondal, I think,' Henri replied in a whisper.

'Korean mafia?' Oberon asked, widening his eyes.

'Don't shout like that. Yes, it just so happens that my close friend has acquaintances there.'

'Is she also from the mafia? Sorry, but normal people rarely have such acquaintances.'

'No. She once stood up for this one guy who was being set upon by a gang of Hong Kong yobs. One of these guys turned out to be the son of the head of a large clan of the Hong Kong Triad and the other – the nephew of the man who runs the entire underground gaming business in Seoul. Alone against four, just with a medical scalpel in hand. The situation was resolved peacefully and since then they respected her very much. She is now quite a famous surgeon, so several big bosses from the Seoul shadow world at once trusted their lives, and the lives of loved ones, exclusively to her. In return, she insisted that they regularly transfer donations to support several orphanages and hospitals.'

'Sorry, but it doesn't sound very believable. Who will go up against the triad gang armed with only one scalpel?' Oberon remarked skeptically.

'I couldn't believe it either. If I hadn't been the guy she stood up for.' Henri held out with a smile.

'As always, you're full of surprises, Monsieur Leroy. By the way, I seem to have finally realized that everything that is happening here isn't a dream, but even so, I still don't understand what's happening.'

'Honestly, I haven't fully figured it out myself. By the way, how long ago did you quit running?'

'It's been a while. I was overwhelmed with work, and my amorous affairs were in full swing. By the way, bridge is primordially Russian game, not British,' Oberon said mockingly.

'Well, at least something doesn't change. We found a Russian trace again.' Henri noted as he approached the coveted place with the cache.

Despite the fairly conscientious packaging, some rainwater had still ended up in the box with the gadgets.

'Oh…' Henri breathed heavily. 'The main thing is whether the walkie-talkie will work.'

Unfortunately, it was completely ruined by the rainwater. The telephone lying underneath showed all the formal signs of life, only the lack of a signal let it down. In principle, the weak connection would be enough for Henri to send the location through the direction finder. Having moved forward a little, Henri came out onto a cliff, from where they had a beautiful view of the lake. Here he caught a weak signal. After sending the location to Jules and Jiwon, he decided that he should start that very unpleasant conversation with Oberon.

'Do you remember when and how you got here?' began Henri, breaking the silence.

'My father and I were preparing for his inauguration. I told him to quit this venture and retire, not that I really believed in these stories with a curse, but just those cases with your uncle and grandfather... Plus your father's accident... It's all so very strange. In few words, we had another altercation and I went to the center to drink a couple of pints of beer in a bar... I woke up in this psychiatric hospital in South Korea.' Oberon squeezed, out looking toward the lake.

'Hmmm... Listen, have you seen the Langlais twins lately?'

'About six months ago at the wedding of Claude and Marie Byron. What are you getting at?'

'Have you seen both? Sister and brother?' Henri asked.

'No, just the sister. Charles, on the other hand, seems to have moved somewhere a hundred years ago. You know, I have a feeling that for the last hour you have been beating around the bush, afraid to tell me something. I'm right?'

'Sorry...' Henri began dropping his eyes. 'I found out quite recently... I... I'm very sorry.'

'No... You don't mean to say... Father... He still passed the initiation? He is sick? What about him?' he asked in a trembling voice.

'Oberon...' Henri continued to turn to him. 'According to the official version, the cause of the fire was a fault in the electrical wiring... No one in the house survived... Monsieur and Madame Bernard... They... Everything most likely happened on the evening when you were kidnapped. I'm so sorry.'

Oberon grabbed his head with his hands and stepped aside with a cry. Henri didn't try to catch up with him. Today he needed to be alone with his pain. Exhaling heavily, he leaned back on the grass, staring at the incredibly beautiful full moon and the huge number of stars scattered across the black sky. This night was full of grief and beauty.

'They will find you.' He heard their red-haired companion say as she decided to settle down next to him on the grass.

'I know. Most likely, we won't have time to do anything about it,' he said turning his head toward her.

The girl silently looked at the night sky.

'Are you scared? Scared of the fact that they are around?' she suddenly asked, still without looking at him.

'Surprisingly, no… For the first time in my life, I'm not scared at all.'

Breathing in the cold air deeply, he savored the view of the sky. They spent the rest of the night in silence. Henri heard Oberon sobbing quietly, unable to contain the pain. Mademoiselle Crane muttered something under her breath. It was rather damp and cold that night, but it was the first night in recent days that Henri finally had no dreams.

***

'Will you wake up on your own or should I call the prince?' opening his eyes, Henri saw the contented grin of his younger brother hanging over him.

Looking around, he noticed Park Jiwon on the phone and a sad Oberon sitting on the ground by a large rock. Judging by the position of the sun, it was now about five in the morning. Henri scanned his surroundings, but could not find the familiar red-haired silhouette nearby.

'Are you looking for someone, big brother?' Jules asked, holding out his hand. Leaning on his younger brother, Henri slowly got up, shaking slightly from mild colic. He back lay down in a dream.

'Our companion, is she already in the car?' Henri asked uncomprehendingly, still looking around.

'Companion?' Jules knitted his eyebrows, adding, 'Are you under the influence of drugs? What did they give you?'

'No, no, there was a girl with us… A pretty red-haired Frenchwoman.,' the elder brother did not calm down.

'Ah, well, since she's pretty, then, of course, it changes things. There were crowds of them walking in the woods last night, but there were only a few cute ones among them,' Jules said ironically.

'How do you like camping in Korea?' Sipping green tea brewed in a thermos, Jiwon approached closer to him.

'Excellent, apart from the wild back pain,' Henri complained, rubbing his lower back and vaguely holding his gaze on his former classmate.

'And what is our alignment now?' Catching Henri's eye, Jules nodded toward Oberon.

'We have victims and witnesses, so now there are more threads in this tangle. This is most likely good.'

'How did you get out of the hospital?' Jiwon began, but a sudden call interrupted her question and she stepped aside to talk.

'Yes, Henri, how did you manage to get out on your own, without a messenger? Sure, you are very strong and independent, but so many cameras and guards,' Jules asked in surprise.

'Without a messenger?' asked Henri.

'Yes. The Jiwon guys said that your contact was found unconscious in the kitchen, someone stunned him from behind.'

'Him?' realizing with fear in which direction the conversation was heading, he asked again.

'Yes, the local doctor... His surname seems to be translated from Japanese as...'

'Crane?' Henri whispered, feeling thousands of daggers of awareness sinking into his head. 'Tsuru... His last name is Tsuru.'

Under the weight of his thoughts, the elder Lero slowly sank to the ground. 'That is, all this time I was wandering around the hospital with a mentally ill woman, most likely diagnosed with schizophrenia, persecution mania, and pyromania. After all, a thousand times, literally at any second she could harm herself or those around her; moreover, I let her walk free so that she could continue to destroy everything around her. The funniest thing is that for the first time in a long time, I was really drawn to someone seriously. As if I felt... I felt something in common with her? Realizing the absurdity of the situation, Henri at first only smiled slightly, but a minute later, he burst into hysterical laughter, forcing even Oberon, who was leaving in the direction of the road to shudder.

'Things are good?' Jules asked him quietly, squatting next to his brother and gently placing his hand on his back.

'Yes, I just…' Unable to contain his laughter, he tried to force himself to calm down. 'I, I… I didn't find that doctor, or rather he found me, but instead of the understandable "Hello, I'm your messenger, sent by Jiwon." He began to read me Japanese hokku as if hinting at, most likely, the following lines with the word "crane," but I wasn't familiar with the work of the Japanese poets, of course, and didn't understand him.'

'I'm so disappointed in you.' Jules chuckled contentedly, nodding to his brother to continue the story.

'So… I came across a patient drawing a crane from the life of a crane-fish, which seemed very symbolic to me.' Henri nodded inquiringly to Jules, wanting to make sure that he was catching what he was talking about.

'Just keep going. I'll understand this later,' the younger brother answered slightly absently, putting his index and middle fingers to his temple.

'So after I saw her drawing of a crane, which I took for a sign, I asked her to help me shut down the hospital, steal Oberon and these sneakers and a sweatshirt, and stun the Peking Opera concert about the Monkey King based on Wu Cheng'en's Journey to the West.'

The shocked Jules, dressed today in light trousers and a beige chunky sweater, exhaled heavily, and sat down next to his brother on the grass. He paused for a little while digesting everything he heard, but then still gave his comment.

'It seems you fell in love.' Before he could finish, they both burst into wild laughter.

'How about a double wedding?' Henri suggested, clutching his stomach.

'Brothers, we have news,' Jiwon called out to them in an agitated voice. 'The guys of Hwang Zhiguk couldn't trace those calls, but since they were international, they managed to get to the account that pays for the connection. It turned out to be offshore, of course, so it took them a long time to show all the payments. As a result, they found a certain Noah Fisher from California, of whom there are more than three hundred in this state. As you understand, it would be incredibly difficult to find the right guy if not for one case…'

Jiwon became very nervous, which made Henri's heart sink into his heels. Jiwon is a surgeon with perfect composure and iron nerves, so if she gets nervous, it really is a serious business.

'That name came up on the police bulletin. Two men were killed. The police say it was an attempted robbery. The criminals tried to hijack a yacht, the owners were inside and resisted. As a result, the yacht was set on fire, and both men died. The first one was killed by the shots. They shot him twice. First, they hit him in the arm; the next shot was through the head. The second man died, choking on the smoke from the fire. It all happened on the island of Avgeman, where one of the victims lived. There are only about three thousand inhabitants, so the case was very quickly made public. The guys found an obituary... I'm not entirely sure, but... Well, look...'

Jiwon held out the phone to Henri with a shaking hand. Turning the screen toward him, he saw the title of the obituary: "A pensioner died at the hands of robbers on his yacht." Below was a description of the ongoing events that Jiwon was talking about. The dead men were brothers and... His gaze dropped lower to the photo of the dead men and for a moment the air he breathed seemed to be stuck somewhere deep in his throat.

'This... this...' Jules, who was sitting next to him, shook his head in horror, unable to accept what his eyes saw.

'No, Jules, it is. In this photo, our father, and uncle.' He exhaled, leaning back on the grass and looking at the sky, which at that moment seemed incredibly heavy to him.

Even though the drive to the hotel was incredibly quiet, the atmosphere inside the car was quite tense. Jiwon decided to defuse the situation by turning on the radio, but quietly, so as not to wake Oberon, who was asleep in the backseat. Jules, sitting next to him, silently turned the watch around his right wrist. He always did this when he was nervous, from their childhood. Seated in the front passenger seat Henri crossed his arms over his chest and admired the view of morning Seoul. His gaze was clear, his breathing was even and only a small tremor of his left hand, which he was masterfully pressing with his right one, betrayed his stress.

The clock was exactly nine in the morning when they arrived at the hotel.

'Guys, thank you so much again. I...' Oberon began breathing deeply. 'I don't know what I would have done if you hadn't saved me. As my old man said, it's better not to cross the road to the men of the Lero family,' he added wearily smiling, opening the salon door.

'Maybe you will come to a restaurant with us and we can have breakfast together?' Jules suggested politely getting out of the car.

'We'll also have breakfast, but in Paris,' Oberon replied, putting his hand on his shoulder.

'By the way, how do you plan to get to Paris? Hitchhiking or by sea in a container? I can call a couple of logisticians I know in this city.' Henri chuckled as he approached them.

'Only if you keep me company,' Oberon retorted, slightly tilting his head to one side. 'I got through to my insurance company and they've already confirmed my identity at the consulate. Tickets for the return flight have been bought, I will leave with a temporary identity card. In half an hour, their man will arrive to bring up all the necessary documents, money, and clothes, plus we will need to discuss the issue with the hospital. I think you understand, this is a delicate matter. They could either be involved in my kidnapping or just thought that I was another patient trying to impersonate someone else,' he finished, putting his hands in his pockets and gazing at the slightly sleepy Henri. 'It's funny… When you're so shaggy, I think about your teenage emo bang. It was stunning.

'Did you hear, Jules? Not everyone considered my teenage emo bang disgusting,' Henri remarked with a significant nod toward his brother.

'Come on, seriously? Did you think it was better that way?' Jules asked, raising his eyebrows in bewilderment.

'Of course better. He looked like a very pretty girl,' Oberon whispered meaningfully in a low voice, winking and causing a sudden fit of unrestrained laughter from the youngest of the Lero brothers.

'You're disgusting.' Henri rapped out with a cold squint.

'Okay. Okay! I confess it was too much,' Oberon corrected himself, smiling and poking the elder Lero in the shoulder. 'But such a pretty person as you should finally learn how to accept compliments,' he continued slyly.

'Why do I have the feeling that we have returned to the days of studying at our boarding school?' Henri answered tiredly, rolling his eyes.

'See you in Paris! I'll wait for you at my wedding inauguration,' Jules said, shaking hands with Oberon.

'Wedding inauguration?' Oberon raised his eyebrows in amazement.

'Yes, it's cheaper. Times are difficult now and renting a hall is an expensive pleasure,' Jules murmured comically.

'Then I'll see you in Paris,' Oberon confirmed, waving at them.

'I won't miss you. Not after the remark about the bang,' Henri finally quipped and the guys returned to the car.

'Why can't he count the strength of his pats? In half a day of communication with him, my shoulders were crippled!' Henri complained, taking off his sweatshirt and showing a large number of bruises on his shoulder under the hospital uniform.

'Oberon? Well, yes. He's a tactile guy. He'd already managed to lightly push me a couple of times, but it didn't seem to me that his hand was heavy. Is it not so?' Jules wondered, looking at his brother's bruises from the back seat. 'This is strange... You didn't annoy him with anything? Or, on the contrary, is this a manifestation of hidden feelings?' commented Jules, grinning, but catching a stern look from Henri immediately added, 'Most likely your skin is thinner than mine, so the bruises on it look bluer.'

'Of course, the bruises on his skin look bluer, because he has blue blood,' Jiwon quipped.

'For this insolence, you will pay for my breakfast, young lady,' Henri threw back at her in the voice of the abbess of a convent.

'듣고있어요. 엄마. (Okay, mother),' Jiwon replied dutifully.

'Don't be impudent to your mother,' the eldest of the Lero brothers grumbled, barely holding back a smile rising from his lips.

'At this rate, by the time he's seventy he'll finally speak Chinese.' Dr. Bak hissed, causing Jules to laugh hysterically and Henri to look displeased.

The fish restaurant they were heading to was only ten minutes away from the hotel. Finding a free parking space nearby wasn't difficult, so fifteen minutes after leaving Oberon the whole company was already awaiting their breakfast.

'So,' Henri began cautiously, 'as we have been able to find out, the curse has overtaken all the heads of families who tried to infringe on the right of the Guardian of the Trust. At the same time, the death of a senior clan member made it possible for a widow-regent or an officially authorized person from the family to take the place at the head of the clan. This person had to be either specially appointed or was the eldest or sole heir. Trying to seize power over management, someone methodically removed first the Guardians from the Kebe family, then the Heads of the founding families of the Trust and their heirs. The number of deaths from each house was approximately the same, not counting the last years... And... Considering what we learned this morning...' Henri looked at the others. 'As wild as it may seem... We all understand what this means.'

'Henri, we don't know anything yet. You can't say that.' Jules reproachfully looked at his older brother, realizing what he was driving at now.

'Jules… You know, I would never think so, but the facts… In the Kebe family, only girls are born for several generations in a row. This gives them the right only to temporary, limited management. Male babies have always died as a result of mysterious miscarriages. Jules, like you, I was convinced all my life that both grandfather and uncle and father – they all became victims, carrying themselves to the slaughter in the name of the future Trust. Well, judge for yourself, Jules, were they stupid enough to throw themselves into the fire so recklessly like moths? The miscarriages on the part of Kebe and the succession of deaths of the heads on the part of our home coincide chronologically. So tell me, Jules, do you think this is just a coincidence?' Henri asked his silent brother, feeling tears coming to his eyes. 'That photo in the obituary… They… They faked their death to deceive everyone else by acting out this circus over and over again.'

'Stop it,' Jules demanded, painfully clenching his fist and looking at Henri's red eyes.

'Everything falls into place when you accept the fact that they did not think of anyone when they went for it. Not about you, not about our mother. They had no particular ideology or any idea. They only did it for the damn money.'

'Stop before it's too late. I beg you.' Jules's usually rather lightface at that moment acquired a crimson tint. In his eyes, red vessels appeared from anger and a tear flowed down his left cheek.

'They didn't think about anyone, not even…about those children from the Kebe family. Boys who weren't born. Do you think all these miscarriages are just a lucky coincidence?' Henri's lips trembled, but he continued to speak through tears. 'Children killed in the womb of Kebe mothers, the parents of Oberon and God only knows how many more ruined souls… They… They… All of them. Grandfather, father and even uncle, and…

'Don't dare! I swear if you dare!' screamed the outraged Jules, jumping up.

'And Thomas…' Henri's eyes became empty for a second. 'Where do you think he is?' Looking up at his younger brother, he continued. 'Do you think that he was also in their secret gang of the living dead? Maybe he laughed softly while I read my fucking poem at his funeral? He was sitting comfortably in the kitchen while we were burying the corpse of his double behind the next wall. Or at that time, he was already slowly drinking bourbon somewhere in

California, along with the rest of the members of this closed club? No, probably he nailed them so that they would no longer try to call us on international lines? That's rather expensive, but he always was so economical…

Without finishing, Henri felt a blow to the jaw of such force that he lost his balance and immediately fell on his back, turning over on the chair. Without waiting for a second push, he got to his feet and immediately responded to his younger brother with a backhand. Henri can hardly be called an athlete, but four years of Wing Chun training in Guangzhou still allowed him to stand up for himself. Strong Jules was a little taken aback by such sharp resistance, but realizing that they had a serious fight, he decided to move to a new level putting all his strength into the next hook. On his failure, Henri managed to dodge and the younger one almost flew into the next table. Jiwon sat at the table slowly sipping strawberry juice from a glass with a reproachful look at Henri. Catching her eye, he immediately answered.

'But this is logical. We must think impartially and Trust the facts.' At this phrase, Henri realized that contrary to all the physical laws of this world, he lifted off the ground with a sudden jolt from the side and for three seconds was flying somewhere to the left side of the hall. Before he had time to enjoy the flight, he landed with pain on something very hard and then felt another pain in his back and elbows. Looking back, he realized that he was lying on the floor in water and fragments of one of the display aquariums for fish served in the restaurant. The water flowing out of the aquarium mixed with the blood flowing from cuts, quickly spreading across the floor. Once in a noisy restaurant silence reigned, and only the sound of small perches twitching fins, convulsively gripping the air with gills, broke the silence.

'Quickly pick up the fish and put them in the other aquariums.' Jiwon snapped in a commanding tone, leaning over and taking one of the carp and moving it to another aquarium display case nearby.

Henri and Jules looked at each other in confusion at first, but after a few seconds, Jules gave his hand to his brother and Henri silently accepted it. Having quickly moved the fish to new homes and cleaned up the blood mixed with fragments from the floor, Henri went to the bathroom to wash his hand. The cuts were shallow but multiple.

'I'll bandage you up. Jiwon gave me some bandages,' Jules called from behind him.

Henri silently turned to his brother and obediently stretched forward his crippled left hand.

'Again the left one,' Jules remarked with a smile, bandaging the cuts.

'Favorite target of my younger brothers,' Henri replied, smiling back. 'Sorry… I just wanted to understand… I was thinking and… I didn't notice how I said it out loud. I've more of a grudge against him. Why did he put all this on himself? You know, I would like to just believe the facts, but Thomas… Good guy Thomas. He was too good for this wrong world.'

'Hmmm…' Jules nodded his head. 'I'm sorry too. I completely forgot that this is not only my grief. It hurt you as much to say it as it hurt me to hear it. I agree that we need to check everything, but do not lose faith in people,' he continued, looking his brother straight in the eyes. 'Faith can see more than eyes and hear more than ears, Henri. As long as we know and remember who Thomas was, we will not go astray, even if the sky above will be hopelessly dark.'

'Sometimes he could certainly be harmful and stubborn, but he always acted according to his conscience. That's how I remember him,' Henri confirmed.

'Me also. Until just now.'

'You know, in recent days I have remembered a lot from my past. Now, it seems to me, it becomes clear why he was on our father's side,' continued Henri leaning on the sink. 'After all, in those days I really was too unstable and fixated on my pain so much that I completely forgot that I was not alone, but we all then lost mother. I dug into the bottom so deep that I did not listen and did not see anything or anyone around. Lack of empathy is a worrying sign. At some point, I really could become dangerous to myself or others.'

'It's hard for everyone to see themselves from the outside. Life is given to us for constant work on ourselves to improve. Although sometimes it seems to me that we are all reborn together with nature every spring,' Jules reasoned aloud as he finished with the dressing.

'Sometimes I feel like I'm reborn every morning,' Henri said with a smile.

'The main thing is that you are reborn as yourself, not as Leopold,' Jules remarked ironically, causing a fit of laughter from his older brother. 'No, I definitely won't survive another meeting with that character.'

Back in the hall, the brothers found Jiwon talking to the owner of the establishment. From the whole conversation, Henri could only make out something about someone's aunt and her three nephews who the owner of the restaurant and Jiwon were quite familiar with. Seeing the brothers, he nodded eloquently and said something unintelligible to Jiwon as he walked away toward the back room.

Approaching the table, Henri looked at Jules, who was nervously spinning his watch around his wrist. Apparently, it wasn't only Henri who was sometimes afraid of Jiwon to the point of making him sick. Even when she is in a state of absolute calm, Dr. Bak still knows how to cause one to shake with fear when she wants. Sipping slowly from a cup of oolong tea, she gazed at the brothers as they sat back down. They did so in silence without touching their cups. Jiwon slowly shifted her gaze from one to the other and silently pulled out two gray folders from her briefcase.

'Before you did ballroom dancing here, I wanted you to take a look at these,' she began, handing them the folders.

Henri slowly peeled back the thin cover and scanned the first page of the printed document. 'So, what do we have here? Diagnosis in Korean...' He noted to himself. 'Epilepsy, convulsion, I can't make out anything further...'

'Jiwon, how did you get hold of Oberon's medical record?' Henri asked with interest.

'This is Jules's record,' she answered, looking into his eyes.

'What do you mean, Jules?' Henri puzzled, looked from his girlfriend to his younger brother.

'Sorry... We didn't want to dump everything on you at once. I was a little unwell in the evening and... And just in case, we went to the hospital,' Jules began guiltily.

'How bad is it?' the elder brother asked, closing the folder with a clap.

'It's no big deal,' Jules continued cautiously, but Jiwon interrupted him immediately.

'Severe convulsion, very similar to epilepsy, then asphyxia after which he simply passed out for almost an hour and a half.'

'Why the hell didn't you say this before?' Henri cried, almost switching to a scream as he jumped up from the table. 'This about MY BROTHER, Jiwon! The only one! I asked you to look after him, so why did I...'

'Sit down.' She snapped, slapping the folder in front of him. 'Sit down and turn the page.'

Exhaling loudly, Henri turned the page and immediately forgot everything he was thinking about a second ago.

'This... This... Is this the aneurysm again?' In front of him was a snapshot of the brain with a noticeable neoplasm in the area of the insular lobe.

'Turn the page,' Jiwon said calmly.

Henri saw an image made using a CT scan. The neoplasm was very large and the outline was unnaturally smooth.

'It looks like a man-made object,' Henri remarked.

'Implanted into the islet lobe, which is responsible for sympathetic and parasympathetic regulation,' Jiwon said.

'Sounds scary,' Jules commented, staring at the picture in amazement.

'This is the regulation of vital processes: respiration, cardiovascular system, musculoskeletal system, behavioral, and emotional responses,' Jiwon explained, slowly lighting a cigarette.

'That is the same place as the aneurysm which was cut out when I was in my teens, so then I get a new one?'

Henri scanned the photo carefully again. Whatever it was, it had a centerpiece and a lot of small ramifications. The main body of the object strongly resembled something in shape...

'I have a feeling that I have a sea angel in my head,' Jules drawled thoughtfully, examining the picture.

'Yes, very similar in form,' agreed Henri, nodding. 'This is a deep-sea clam with an almost completely transparent body. They inhabit the waters of the Arctic Ocean,' he added, catching Jiwon's questioning gaze.

'Can we cut it out?' Jules offered with a shrug.

'There are only a dozen neurosurgeons all over the world working in the field of implanting such complex devices, two of whom are no longer alive,' Jiwon reasoned, absentmindedly looking at the picture.

'And at least five of them we simply cannot trust, because one of them, most likely, was the one who put it in you,' Henri stated, rubbing the bridge of his nose.

'And there's no hope for the remaining three since they are considered to be professionally written off,' Jiwon finished, spreading her hands and exhaling heavily.

'Not three. Two,' Henri remarked with a smile.

'Laocoon? Are you serious? He's crazy!' Dr. Bak said, raising an eyebrow skeptically.

'If anyone should be trusted in our turbulent times, it's the madmen,' Henri said with sparkling eyes, putting the folder aside. 'There are about thirty corporations in the world that have the necessary resources to manufacture this kind of neurochip, but as far as I know, only five of them were researching in a similar direction.' Henri looked from Jules to Jiwon. 'And I find it surprisingly strange that I'm working in one of them.' He lowered his empty glass down on the table with a bang and continued with his head down. 'Funny, isn't it? I blindly believed that I had retired from all the affairs of the Trust, leaving it all to our aunt in Hong Kong. But how blind I was…' he whispered sadly, and then laughing. 'I didn't seem to go anywhere.'

'But didn't our aunt leave the family?' Jules wondered.

'Only for a diversion,' concluded Henri. 'Most likely, they have been playing fake deaths with this device for the last twenty years. It first causes reactions similar to the curse, then slows down all life processes in the body to a minimum, creating the illusion of death. By the way, this explains why I did not have an aneurysm, unlike all the other family members – since I left home at fourteen and gave up the inheritance the operation was useless.'

'And how do you explain the rest of the cases, before the chip? Operations related to aneurysms began to be performed in our family not so long ago, after the death of our grandfather, if I'm not mistaken.' Jules noted.

'Checkmate. I have no idea yet,' Henri admitted spreading his hands.

'Will you be able to get a sample?' Jiwon interrupted their thoughts.

'Yes, I'll go to the airport right now,' Henri said, getting up.

'I'm with you,' said Jules, standing up.

'Wait. Whoever has implanted this device in you, I believe that it isn't only there for aesthetics. In other words, you'll be tracked within two minutes,' Jiwon continued anxiously.

'How about a plug?' Jules suggested immediately.

'The disappearance of the GPS signal from the tracker will automatically notify the "big brother" who is tracking us about an attempt to hide the location,' Henri said. 'Alternatively, we can use a spoofer. Thus, we will not drown the signal but will generate additional false requests. We'll make you a transmitter, but we will have to fly in a private plane, because we'd not be allowed to take a toy like that on board an ordinary airline,' he concluded. 'Jiwon, can you help me get it?'

'I'll ask the guys to bring it to the airport,' she said, pulling out her phone.

'Well! Let's hit the road?' Jules responded enthusiastically as he walked out into the courtyard.

'Just like that in a straitjacket?' Jiwon asked Henri, who was still wearing his hospital uniform.

He slowly examined himself and only then realized that he was still dressed in the hospital uniform that strongly resembled pajamas. On top of that, his clothes were splattered with his blood.

'Oh. We'll stop by the store on the way and I'll try to get into the shower at the airport. There should be a VIP zone or a hotel,' Henri answered shyly, rubbing his dirty sleeve.

'Well, we'll hardly meet Italian tailors here on our way to the airport, but I know a couple of places. Okay, I'll call some guys about the spoofer,' Jiwon reported and waved to the owner as she left the restaurant.

Henri looked around. Everything in the restaurant was the same as when they had arrived: several groups of people actively discussing something in the right corner, a couple of lovers cooing at the next table, a waitress slowly wiping empty tables with a red rag, fresh-water carp that seemed to have forgotten about their recent relocation. Everything quickly returned to its previous state, as if there nothing had happened. As if they had never been here.

Putting his hand in his pocket, he felt there the anime figure left for him by Thomas. It had accompanied him all this week.

'Well, buddy,' he whispered, tightening his fingers around the figure. 'The next station is Taibei.'

Chapter 6
Turtle

'I've always talked about the inversely proportional relationship between the size of the car and the complexes of their owners,' complained Henri, sitting in the front passenger seat of the rented car sipping from a plastic bottle of carefully stored Seoul makgeolli.

'Oh well, forgive me, but all the rusty bicycles for rental have already been dismantled and I had to force Your Highness to get into this wretched BMW,' Jules answered as he turned off the highway.

'BMW of what?' blinking his eyes, asked the elder brother.

'Some kind of X5 model, I think. You know, I'm not particularly disposed toward cars either. Oh, if you and I sat on old mopeds…' The younger man began nodding.

'Yes! And the chicest thing is to ride it with a rain cape and high-heels like the local ladies.' Chuckled Henri. 'Oh-oh-oh, Jules, turn it up! This is Teresa Teng! 你问我爱你有多 深, 我爱你 有几分 (you asked how deep my love for you is, how much I love you), 我的情也真, 我的爱也 真.月亮代表我的心 (and my feelings are real, and my love is real, the moon represents my heart),' Henri sang sincerely to the radio.

'I don't know what the song is about, but I'm sure you misinterpreted half of the words.' Giggled Jules. 'That's it. Stop singing! Either you sing, or Teresa goes. I'm serious.'

'轻轻的一个吻, 已经打动我的心 (one light kiss has already touched my heart).' Henri howled without letting go.

'Buddy, are you sure that we don't need to go to the main office in Taiwan, research center, or one of the buildings in the technopark?' Jules asked, carefully following the road. It was very cloudy, plus it gets dark rather early here. Thus in less than half an hour, driving would become difficult.'

'There are no details for practically for 67%, even the technical task or application for this project formally does not exist. Based on this situation, one of the warehouses is more suitable for us. Most likely, the one where the products are more expensive will suit us, because this is a good trick to justify more security on the territory. It's good that we came on holiday. In theory, most of the staff was supposed to go to relatives.'

'And what about the remaining 33%?' Jules asked his brother jokingly.

'It's likely that the country or company was chosen incorrectly,' Henri replied calmly.

'Oh… Well then, we practically win. You reassure me,' the younger man quipped.

'And now the fun part,' Henri continued, turning the radio down. 'We're passing your beloved Jiufen.'

'Beloved? Well, how can this city be my beloved if I…' And in that instant when they drove onto the main road around the bend, Jules was speechless with the blinding beauty of it all.

'Jiufen…' Of course, how could he have forgotten. This is the same incredible town in northeastern Taiwan, once founded by the nine families (九份 translates as "nine parts"). The same Jiufen, included in the top 25 most beautiful small cities in the world. The same Jiufen, which became the prototype of the famous phantom city from the immortal masterpiece of Japanese animation, "Spirited Away," which was beloved by both the brothers.

'The main thing is not to eat anything here,' the enchanted Jules remarked with a smile, recalling the plot of the aforementioned work.

'It's a shame because you could turn in to a very cute piggie and I would get a job at the local baths and save you.' Henri noted busily, taking several photographs.

'You would be so carried away by the optimization of existing business processes in these baths that I would have to build a brick house, like Naff-Naff, to survive,' the blond man drawled plaintively.

'Oh, you! You don't know me at all! This isn't the factor that would make me forget about your stigma,' Henri insisted while adjusting the focus of the phone camera.

'And the lady bathers?' Jules smirked with a significant wink.

'You can't fool your own blood.' The elder brother nodded in agreement, checking the route using the GPS navigator. 'About 20 more minutes and we'll be there. Let's take a quick look at our tactics again.'

'You'll set up the system remotely, and then transmit a signal to your friend Lu Su in Hong Kong. Su hacks into their system, gives us the coordinates of the sample's location and an electronic ID card to enter the building. By the way, are you sure you're still friends? You took his girlfriend away from him this spring?'

'You got it all wrong, she was not his girlfriend. By the way, the number of "girlfriends in his mind" is approximately equal to the population of an average European state. I would have to declare celibacy if I could not look at those on whom he laid his cunning eye. And by the way, we seem to have moved away from the topic.'

'Okay. This means that we enter the building as quickly as possible, take a sample and leave. At the entrance, you show your working ID card, but you attach it along with the phone, which will have an electronic ID specialist with the right to enter. Introduce yourself as French professor Lero from the company's Hong Kong R&D center. I'll call myself your graduate student assistant.' Jules rapped out in the voice of an excellent student.

'Not bad, but plan B?' said Henri, preparing the computer for connection to the network.

'Are we pretending to be stupid foreigners in search of free Wi-Fi?' answered Jules, naively flapping his eyelashes.

'That's plan C. And plan B is to de-energize the facility and play night spies,' he explained, briskly tapping his fingers on the glove compartment.

'We're on the spot. Call Lu Su while I get the license plates off the car,' Jules commanded, turning off the engine and stopping about two hundred meters from the base.

Henri checked the settings one last time and immediately reached for the satellite phone tucked away in the car's glove compartment.

'Su, we're starting. Seize the signal as I can establish a connection. Just a second… Jules is here, I'll turn on the speakerphone.'

'How are you, blondie?' Lu Su asked the younger Lero in a mocking tone.

'Not bad, skinny, but I have a persistent feeling that something will go wrong. I, of course, do not see anything in the dark, but offhand this area is too large for a warehouse. By the way, we passed Jiufen!' Jules, with a strange mixture of delight and anxiety in his voice, recounted the latest events.

'I hope you didn't stop there for dinner? Although Henri is asleep and sees himself in the role of the protagonist of "Spirited Away,"' Su said cynically.

'And Su, of course, would be the dragon boy who ended up saving this girl, who is saving her family. Here is such a vicious circle of heroism,' the elder Lero grumbled, adding, 'I'm connecting now.'

'By the way, about my charm. How is Jiwon doing?' Lu Su asked flirtatiously. 'Did she ask about me?'

'No,' Henri said sternly. 'By the way, she changed her phone number again because of you,' he commented with a smile.

'Like a real Confucian husband, I restrain myself as best I can, so I try not to bother the lady. It is you French who throw compliments at everyone,' Lu Su said jokingly.

'No, Su, not all French. Only my brother,' said Jules, bursting into laughter with the young man on the line.

'I will be above all this and will simply ignore your envy,' Henri replied diligently holding back a smile.

Their primary task was to scan the system for vulnerabilities since it was necessary to understand what kind of object was in front of them, without the unnecessary need to connect with Lu Su's guys. It would be incredibly careless for them to give away the fact that they were familiar with cyber intruders. Henri decided to scan the network using one of the pirated counterparts of the Nmap utility with V-A parameters.

'How's it going, Paris?' Su asked, breaking away from the vivid debate with Jules about the main advantages of Taiwanese cuisine.

'You know, Zhengzhou...' Henri began.

'Su, I didn't know you were from Zhengzhou!' Jules was surprised.

'I am originally from Hefei, which is in Anhui province, but when I was twelve, my whole family moved to Zhengzhou. You should visit us during the Spring Festival (Chinese New Year). I will introduce you to my grandfather. He's one hundred and eight years old next year.'

'A year ago, you said that he was one hundred and four,' Henri quipped.

'He's aging quickly; after a hundred it's like two years for everyone. Thus you better come to see him faster,' Su added with a smile.

'I'm living my whole life just like your grandfather, so...' Henri began, but in the same second, he suddenly fell silent.

'What's there? What do you see?' Su asked carefully.

Henri exhaled deeply, then sent the screenshot to Su and slowly leaned back in his chair to await his reaction.

'Oh, oh, oh, oh. x, x. This warehouse... It's...' He gasped heavily, having received the image that Henri had sent.

'How fast will the guys be able to cope?' continued Henri, calming his trembling left hand.

'Given the scale... Two hours. I'll ask them to start right now,' Su said quickly, judging by the sound, he began typing something quickly.

'Guys, what's the matter? Please explain in laymen's terms so I can understand,' the younger brother requested, as he looked blankly at the data on the screen.

'We're dealing with an automated information telecommunications system that includes several user interfaces for control and means of transmission, processing, and storage of information, as well as finished hardware elements of automation such as sensors, controllers, and actuators based on industrial SCADA protocols,' explained Henri.

'I asked for a simple explanation,' the blond begged, rolling his eyes.

'This is not a warehouse, Jules. This is a special industrial facility, with an area of up to a thousand square kilometers, parts of which can be scattered anywhere. Simply put, I'm not sure that we will be able to pierce this shell,' Henri said, looking at the screen, spellbound.

'The shell of this turtle is too big for conflict inside one family and even for conflict between clans inside the Trust. Don't you think so?' said Jules, turning the watch on his hand again.

'I agree. We'd better not go in there. Let's wait here for two hours until Lu Su's guys can get into the system and at least find out something.'

'If they find some drawings and technical tasks for this chip, then we'll not need a physical sample, 3D models will be enough. Try to sleep, I'll drop you in an hour. We'll have another important destination before we go to Paris. By the way, as far as I understood from the conversation with Jiwon, everything stands?'

'Yes, even my palms are sweating. I'm still surprised at how Jiwon managed to organize everything so quickly, after you came up with this idea.

By the way, is there any regret about your decision?' Jules asked, as he poked his brother in the side with his elbow.

'This is temporary, especially since I am overconfident in my charm,' Henri replied unflaggingly.

'You're incorrigible. You'd better take a nap yourself and I'll stay on duty.'

'Okay. I have a downloaded volume of the science fiction novel, M31,' Henri whispered contentedly, opening the app for reading books on his smartphone and handing it to Jules.

'Ricky Ren? Who is this? Do you have something from Asimov's or Clark's stories?' Jules responded with a skeptical nod.

'It's a good book, I don't understand your skepticism. What's your problem with Ricky Ren?' Spreading his hands in misunderstanding the older brother didn't calm down.

'I just don't like all these "fashionable" authors,' Jules answered honestly.

'Fashionable? Nobody reads it at all, except me. I know a guy who knows him personally. So, he told me that Ricky Ren is a hermit who's been living somewhere on Mount Kailash in Tibet for the last ten years,' the eldest of the children Lero babbled excitedly, putting the computer aside and emotionally depicting the mountain with his hands.

'You scare me a lot at times. Everything as our father said,' whispered Jules and began to read.

'What did he say?' Henri asked curiously.

'Try to sleep, buddy. I hope that the book won't be so boring that it sends me off to sleep,' whispered Jules with a smile, having just received a pinch on the right side from the sleepy Henri.

"You know, I slept so well on the ground that..." Henri managed to say, but his eyes closed at the same second.

Trying to open his eyes forcibly, he felt a blinding light through his eyelids. The first thing he saw was a clear blue sky. Henri lay in front of a large lake with his head thrown back. Looking around he saw a woman with a long blond braid sitting with her back to him. *How beautiful...* thought Henri. 'Hmmm... Mom?' He stood up reaching out to her with his hand and saw that his wrist was now the size of a small garden apple.

'Yes, my love.' The woman half turned around to look at him with such warmth that he would never have confused her face with anything else even after thousands of years. It was the face of his mom.

Gently moving toward her, he laid his head on her lap so that he could feel the touch of her slightly protruding belly. This must be a memory of those times when their mother was in the first stages of pregnancy with Jules.

'Is everything okay, baby?' she asked with a smile.

'I… I… I love you so much,' Henri whispered, barely holding back the tears.

'I know. We're family. Love makes us a family,' she said, gently, stroking the baby's head.

They sat by the lake, silently watching as a pair of ducks floated peacefully past them on its surface.

'Mom… I'm afraid that I won't be able to protect him,' he whispered, putting his hand on her bulging tummy.

'He's a strong, kid. As strong as you and Thomas. The main thing is to believe in each other and to be there for each other,' she replied after kissing the top of Henri's head.

'Sure,' Henri agreed, nodding. 'Jules can handle it.'

'Jules?' Mom smiled.

'Yes, Jules, like Jules Verne.' He smiled back.

'Well, hello, Jules.' She smiled, stroking her belly.

'Jin-jin…' Henri heard the quiet bell of a fishing rod standing alone by the lake. It was stuck halfway into the ground and a bicycle bell tied to it announced the presence of a catch.

'Well, my love, it's time. You should go and check what's there.' Mom turned to him, pointing to the fishing rod.

Henri slowly got to his feet, assiduously brushing the grass off his shorts. Approaching the shore, he felt the rising wind on his bare ankles.

'Come on, dear,' she said encouragingly, seeing his confusion.

Having taken the remaining few steps to the cherished fishing rod, Henri felt his legs give way.

'Jin-jin…' The fishing rod continued to ring, the line of which was tightening more and more with each click, demonstrating the strength of the fish sitting there now – under the water.

'Jin-jin!' Henri timidly grabbed the rod, trying to pull it out of the ground by the handle, but failed. A jolt, one more, but the handle did not give him in any way.

'Mom, she seems to be…' Henri turned but saw only the empty shore of the lake.

'Mom…' Removing his right hand from the rod, he called her again. He was already half-turned, but he immediately felt a strong jerk from under the water – such force that the handle instantly jumped out of the ground, and the whole fishing rod, together with Henri still hanging on was jerked under the water. Within a second, he'd already had his face beaten against the hard surface of the lake, with a loud clap, cutting it with a crash with his nose.

'Tyrts-ts-ts-ts…' Opening his eyes, he saw a huge bullet mark on the windshield of the car, directly opposite his left eye. The bullet pierced only the top layer of what appeared to be bulletproof glass.

'Henri, I'm still dreaming, or is it…' Jules, who had just woken up was immediately interrupted.

'Tyrts-ts-ts-ts…' Another shot hit the car's glass, this time at the level of his nose.

'I'm calling Su,' Henri shouted as he dialed.

'Tyrts-ts-ts-ts…' The third shot, now somewhere at the level of Jules's right eyebrow.

'I seem to remember the name of the model. This is the BMW X5 Security Plus. It's armored.' The younger breathed with relief.

'It is very nice that you just now remembered this.' Henri noted ironically. 'We won the lottery today. I've never been so lucky before.'

'Well, except with Christine Levon in the eighth grade. She was so spectacular, I still don't understand how she pecked at you,' Jules quipped, putting on the bulletproof vest prudently prepared by the Jiwon guys who were now holding it out to his second brother. 'By the way, in vain did we refuse them. It's good that Jiwon insisted.'

'Su, I didn't want to bother you ahead of time…' Henri began.

'Tyrts-ts-ts-ts! Tyrts-ts-ts-ts!' Two more shots, this time somewhere in the hood of the car.

'So that's it. How are the guys doing? We're just getting a little shelling here,' Henri said innocently as if it were a game of golf.

'Oh, guys, it's too early. It's just data lakes! At the moment, I can only say the approximate coordinates of the required laboratory. I'll give you a location and an electronic ID to open all the entrance doors, but you also need an emergency lock code so that you can lock yourself in the laboratory during the search. We'll get it in five minutes. Then we'll act according to the situation. With more information, I'll be able to get you out by roundabout routes, or through ventilation system,' Lu Su continued in a calm tone.

'Tyrts-ts-ts-ts, Tyrts-ts-ts-ts, Tyrts-ts-ts-ts!' A new volley of shots hit the windshield, again at eye level.

'I got the coordinates,' Henri reported, entering the data into the car's navigator.

'Tyrts-ts-ts-ts, Tyrts-ts-ts-ts, Tyrts-ts-ts-ts, Tyrts-ts-ts-ts!' The shots were so frequent that they already sounded like a hailstorm.

'Stop, Henri... Let's just leave, this is crazy!' Jules began.

'But where should we go?' asked the elder of the brothers, looking into Henri's.

'Tyrts-ts-ts-ts! Tyrts-ts-ts-ts! Tyrts-ts-ts-ts! Tyrts-ts-ts-ts!' The sounds of bullets piercing the top layer of the protective glass rumbled non-stop while the brothers silently looked at each other, realizing how recklessness this was, but at the same time, they needed some follow-up measures.

'So, run?' Jules breathed wearily.

'Straight to the laboratory,' Henri confirmed. 'Just turn on the studio version of the track "Roaring Baikal," otherwise I won't give five stars for the trip.'

'Do you still listen to eco punk?' The younger was perplexed, entering the name of the desired track into the search engine.

'What's so surprising about that? If the governments of most countries are still not able to protect nature under their control, then who else can she hope for? Give us an eco-revolution!'

'Tyrts-ts-ts-ts! Tyrts-ts-ts-ts!' Bullets rattled on the hood again.

'You delight me and frighten me at the same time.' Jules breathed heavily. 'Are you sure about all this?' I have two more days left; I'll figure something out.

'Not you, but we have two days in reserve,' Henri corrected him, releasing the handbrake off the car and clinging to the handrail above the door.

'Well then let's go!' under the hail of another batch of shots, Jules shouted, pushing the gas pedal to the limit. The car jerked sharply, accelerating to a hundred kilometers per hour in almost eight seconds.

The rumble of bullets didn't stop and all that Henri could think about was that Lu Su's guys could get the blocking code as soon as possible, otherwise, even if they get to the laboratory they'd be finished. There was very little left before the collision with the lattice gate of a rather impressive size. The main thing now was that their speed was sufficient.

'Jules, I hope you forgot about the brake for a while. Now we need full throttle,' Henri said cautiously.

'The brakes were invented by cowards,' Jules answered, smiling and speeding up.

Only five meters, three meters, one meter remained to the gate… A strong push against the gate slowed down their movement a little, but after a moment they flew over the mainline of fire. Now they had to traverse only seven hundred meters to get to the desired building. The glass at this point was so obscured that it was necessary to navigate exclusively by the data from the navigator.

'Monsieur Lou, how is it with the lock code?' Henri turned to him hopefully.

'Just a minute.'

Having reached the desired building, the guys, taking with them a computer and Jules's transmitter, moved toward one of the entrances to the building. Approaching the reader, Henri brought the electronic ID on his smartphone to the lock, and, to their delight, the door immediately opened.

'Further on minus the first, it's on the stairs to the right,' shouted Henri, looking at the screen.

Moving as fast as possible, the brothers finally found the entrance to the desired laboratory.

'40 * 7143 # 74 * 006,' Henri whispered while entering the code. the door was immediately unlocked.

'Who are you and what are you doing here?' asked the guard in broken English, having appeared out of nowhere, but realizing that there were foreigners in front of him.

'We're from a research center.'

'We're tourists.'

The brothers said, both answering at the same time in English, which made the guard look at them suspiciously as if they were a couple of idiots.

'Yes, I can see it by your bulletproof vests. Put your hands behind your heads,' he commanded, pointing his service pistol at them.

'Calm down, buddy. We'll not shoot near the laboratory,' Henri began carefully coming closer to him, instinctively shielding his brother.

'Stay away,' the guard warned. 'I'll shoot.'

'Jules, I'll distract him and you run to the laboratory,' Henri whispered in French.

'No, I'm not going anywhere without you, especially since it's pointless without a lock code,' the younger replied, also in French.

'Stop talking,' the guard interrupted them in English. 'On your knees and hands behind your heads. Both!'

'Okay, okay,' Henri replied. 'You just…' At that very second, the light in the corridor went out and the fire alarm went off.

Taking advantage of the moment, the guys quickly rushed out of the laboratory door while the guard was momentarily disoriented, but after three seconds he still managed to fire a couple of shots after them.

'Henri, are you there? Get the lock code,' Su shouted into the phone, which was still on speakerphone.

Recovering himself, Henri entered the code into the doors' control panel and the entrance to the laboratory was blocked from external intrusions. The door looked trustworthy, so they seemed to have won some time.

'Everything is fine? We barely had time to turn off the lights and turn on the fire alarm,' Lu Su said from the phone. 'So, wait a minute, I'll get the lighting back for you.'

The lamps that had switched off gave them a view of two floors of the laboratory. The first floor was occupied by an open area with desks for employees and side rooms. The second floor was half-empty, its central part was absent, opening onto a view of the first, with several rather large offices located at the edges.

'So, let's start with the second floor? I'll take the right side, and you…' began the elder brother.

'Henri, what's wrong with your finger?' Jules whispered in fright, tearing a piece of his sleeve from his shirt.

Henri looked at his hands and…oh-oh-oh! As you might guess, the long-suffering left hand was in trouble again. The palm and fingers were covered with blood. Bringing the wrist closer to his face, Henri realized that one of the bullets that the guard had fired at him had grazed his little finger, tearing off a piece on the right side of the middle phalanx, but fortunately only glancing off the bone.

'The costs of the profession. We're spies now,' Henri remarked with a laugh.

'I would say criminals, but let's be romantics. Spies sounds better,' Jules replied, bandaging his finger.

'The laboratory is now in fortress mode; all entrances are tightly closed and can only be opened from the inside. All rooms inside the laboratory must be open. According to the standard scenario, specialists from the central office will soon be engaged in a siege of the fortress, but this will take them at least ten minutes. Thus, we have five minutes to search and five minutes to prepare for departure,' Henri instructed, brushing the overgrown bangs from his eyes.

'I'm embarrassed to ask what we have for an exit plan?' Jules remarked hopefully.

'I'm ashamed to answer that there are only two outputs so far, but even there, fans will most likely be waiting for us. There is also an exit to the roof, but it will be problematic to get out without a helicopter. It would be best to go down two floors to the warehouse, and from there go to the next building, where on the minus fourth floor there is an exit to the underground parking. The alignment is not the worst. Rather, you have four minutes to do the job,' Lu Su commanded over the speakerphone, and the guys dispersed to search on different sides of the floor.

After finding a working computer, Henri installed a couple of spyware flash drives so Lu Su's guys could scan the network faster. Having walked around almost all the rooms, Henri had not seen anything interesting in them, until his attention was attracted by a single closed door, directly opposite the main entrance, through which they got to the floor.

'Su, where is the second exit?' asked Henri curiously.

'On the first floor of the laboratory, between the third and fourth sections,' Su replied showing some interest.

'Is there a code for a room in the center of the second floor, right in front of the main entrance?' Henri asked hopefully.

'Hmmm… Judging by the plan, there are no rooms in the center on the second floor of the laboratory… What type of lock?'

'Electronic…' Henri answered in bewilderment.

'Any ideas?' Su asked hopefully.

'Well… I'll pop the touchscreen module with something, see what we can do. I'll go and get a screwdriver somewhere, and at the same time run along the first floor.' Henri rushed like a bullet to the iron spiral staircase connecting the floors.

The main space on the ground floor was occupied by a common open area, dotted with an endless number of research workstations. On the left edge, there were two meeting rooms. The right side of the floor was occupied by a server room and two small laboratories in which he, fortunately, was able to get a small Phillips screwdriver. He found nothing more interesting than a couple of new prototype exoskeletons and standard corporate eye prostheses.

'Henri,' the voice of his brother interrupted his nostalgia for work, 'run here quickly, I've found something.'

In an instant, flying through the entire hall, Henri quickly climbed to the second floor and the first thing he saw was…the open door of the previously closed room opposite. But how?

'Jules?' Henri called him cautiously.

'Come here quickly.' He heard his brother's voice coming from the previously closed room.

Carefully entering the door, Henri felt confused.

'Jules, how are you…' he began, but immediately froze in place.

In front of his eyes, inside a glass case in the center of the room, stood stands with two types of samples. The first of these, without any doubt, was a prototype of the very chip that was somehow implanted in Jules's brain. The design was somewhat more complicated than they imagined from the photographs, since the number of thin processes from the main part exceeded all their expectations several times over. The second sample was a small rectangular gray box measuring about seven by thirteen centimeters.

'I'm taking both samples.' Jules threw to his brother.

'Okay. I'll check to see if there is anything of value here.'

'Guys, you have one minute, and then come to the transition to the minus third floor.' Lu Su urged them on.

After downloading a couple of programs from a flash drive and stuffing several folders with drawings in his jacket pocket, Henri turned to his brother.

'Well, are you ready?'

'Yes, I hope it's not rush hour there,' Jules replied, exhaling.

'We'll check it very soon. By the way, how did you get in here?' asked Henri, leaving the room and heading for the spiral staircase.

'The door wasn't locked,' Jules answered, shrugging his shoulders.

'Not locked?' Henri asked, raising his eyebrows in surprise, frozen on the penultimate step of the spiral staircase leading to the open area of the first floor.

'Yes,' Jules, who overtook his brother, answered shortly. 'Amazingly, they did not install an additional lock,' he added, turning his head slightly, already almost reaching the transition to the minus third floor.

'Yes... Very much,' Henri whispered, still standing on the stairs connecting the floors. Once again raising his eyes to the very door that was closed two minutes ago, he stepped over the last step and hurried after his brother.

'Are you at lock?' Su asked them briefly.

'Yes, please remind me again, what is there on the minus third floor? The younger man asked politely.'

'Warehouse area, Mario brothers. Jump over the boxes, collect coins, and then go to the parking lot at minus four, in search of the princess. The difficulty is minimal,' Su replied, slowly eating his dinner.

'It seems to me, at the very moment when your friend's life is hanging by a thread from a deadly threat, you are brazenly scoffing something?' Henri was indignant.

'It's a nervous stress seizure. And for supper, there was only tea with milk left,' Mr. Lou replied calmly.

'I hope this is regular tea with milk and you didn't go to Little Lab without me?' Henri continued indignantly. 'I'm absent for a week, and he went straight to the bar!'

'Bar? For milk tea? Are you talking about HK Tea Time? The bar that makes milk tea with twelve-year-old whiskey?'

'Yes, plus homemade milk syrup and two kinds of beers on top,' Su added lovingly. 'Oh yes, the code is 48 * 20849 # 16 * 37208. You have ten seconds after entering until the door automatically locks for ten minutes.'

The brothers looked at each other and entered the code. After a couple of flights of stairs connecting the floors, they finally found themselves in a storage room at minus three. A huge number of boxes were neatly lined up in endless rows, carefully marked with signs on the floor. The ceilings in this block were impressive, about twenty meters high. The boxes supporting them with a flat wall created a kind of giant labyrinth.

'We need a red thread now, Ariadne,' Henri whispered into the phone, looking around.

'The door is in block F-9 and you are now in block A-54. You need to go to the opposite side of the hall to your right. After you find yourself on the right side, walk along the right wall to the end of the hall there should be a path to the end of block C. From block C to block D, there is a passage along a spiral staircase. Then again, head all the time straight along the right wall to the fork between buildings E and F. Then turn into building F, once there walk to the end of the corridor along the left wall to block F-9. Nothing complicated, just like a walk in the park,' having sipped his tea, the satisfied Lu Su finished.

'I'm wondering if I did get up to date that Irish woman, would you rattle it off even faster?' whispered senior Lero into the phone, following to the right wall of the hall.

'Of course not, I would just say it all in Chinese,' Su countered, accompanied by an unkind laugh from Jules.

'By the way, you are the main reason why I never learned it. It's like a mixed marriage. Why do you need to learn a foreign language if your wife speaks it perfectly?' Henri grumbled.

'Oh, how we started talking! Only where, then, is the ring on my finger that has not appeared for all these six years,' said Su, mocking, but capriciously playing along.

'Patience is the highest virtue,' Henri said with a smile.

'But I categorically disagree. Just remember your father. Within two weeks of meeting our mother, and two months of living together – and voila! Marriage and three children are ready,' Jules grumbled actively gesturing.

'They call it fate,' Su explained. 'According to legend, the old man, Yuelao, owns the threads of human destinies. Two red threads of fate tie up the ankles of people bound by it, so there are no obstacles and circumstances that the red thread of fate could not overcome. Even time and distance are powerless in front of her.'

'Bandaging your ankles? Aren't the little fingers tied?' Jules raised his eyebrows in surprise.

'No little fingers are associated with the Japanese version of the legend,' Su replied as the chief expert.

'But sometimes the thread can become stretched or... A little tangled?' asked Henri, giggling mockingly.

'But it will never break,' stated Su.

'And again there is fatalism all around,' Henri remarked, turning around the next row.

'But what, then, the words of Iamblichus that the power of fate extends only to the second lower soul, while a pure soul can be freed with the help of theurgic actions?' Jules deftly remarked.

'Is love above law and fate?' Henri asked with a smile.

'Yes, if we understand God as Love,' Jules agreed.

'Are you siblings?' Su said skeptically.

'Yes. It's just that a white stork brought Jules and my parents found me in a wine barrel,' Henri replied, stopping right in front of the spiral staircase to block D.

'Elders need to yield,' Jules issued, politely letting him go first with the semblance of curtsy as he passed.

'Su, we are in building D. How are things going to the minus fourth floor?' asked Henri.

'Another minute. By the way, you could handle it yourself. They have interface in C ++,' Su said sarcastically.

'I have never called your beloved "Python" a flawed language, I just said "very simplified," so stop being offended,' Henri justified himself, spreading his hands in bewilderment.

'Yes, yes, of course,' Su repeated offended, stroking his mustache that looked like it was turning into a beard.

'He's very vulnerable. A pure techie, you know,' Henri said to his younger brother, covering the phone with his hand.

'So, catch the code: 46 * 20222 # 6 * 14569. Are you already at the door?' Su asked, tightening the samurai tail at the back of his head.

'Yes, we went through the whole labyrinth. But so far, never having met the Minotaur.' Jules noted as he entered the code.

'Oh, it remains only for us to borrow a car from the parking lot and then we can safely leave the building.' Henri breathed.

'How many should there be? In the parking lot?' Jules specified.

'At least ten. Two of them must patrol the perimeter and another five must go in search of us, that is, at least three more cars must remain in the parking lot. At least according to the instructions, they were obliged to leave three cars in case of an emergency evacuation. Unless the security leadership considered this case a force majeure. Although, according to internal instructions, an earthquake, typhoons, and...'

'And?' entering into an empty parking lot, Jules specified.

'And the terrorist threat... But this situation does not formally fall into this category. Nobody seems to care much that we are unarmed. Does anyone ever read instructions?' Henri was indignant.

'It seems that no one but us does,' said Jules sympathetically as he patted his brother on the shoulder. 'The situation is generally non-standard. Let's start with the fact that they started shooting at us without really understanding why we parked near the building.'

'Don't panic. There are cars on autopilot. I'll try to hack one of those that are now patrolling the perimeter and send it to you,' Su reassured them.

'I've always believed in you. I have two bottles of vintage cognac from the family reserve,' Henri said, perking up.

'You won't get off with cognac,' Su responded, removing his hands from the keyboard. 'I need Jiwon's new phone number,' he demanded.

'Jules, it seems we will have to stay here for a while.' Henri turned to his brother, desperately throwing up his hands.

'I agree,' the younger man responded immediately. 'I'm much less afraid of these guys than Jiwon.'

'Well, with you only the beginning of the number and the last three digits I will guess myself. This will remove some of the blame from you,' Su suggested.

Henri rubbed his chin thoughtfully, then looked at Jules and finally said: 'Deal!'

'Well!' Su responded, immediately starting to type something.

'This guy is just a born diplomat,' Henri commented in French, clutching the phone with his palm. 'He always knows what time it is best to ask a particular question and always gets what he wants.'

'But not with Jiwon,' Jules said sarcastically.

'This is a clash of the titans,' Henri replied with a chuckle.

'I don't hear you dictating her number to me,' Su whispered and judging by his voice, he was smiling.

'I don't hear the noise of the car engine,' Henri responded.

'Delivery in two minutes, a red Volvo 5376 KE is on its way to you,' Monsieur Lu said in the voice of the dispatcher, rubbing his beard contentedly.

'Well, let's open the way to retreat. Su, do you have access to drone cameras? Is there anyone ten meters away from our BMW now?' clarified Jules.

'No, it's clean there. Most of the guards are at the gate,' he said in response.

'Okay, then it's time for a pyro show,' Jules whispered with a smile, pressing a button on a small remote control, which he took from his left trouser pocket.

'Piroshow?' Su asked in surprise.

'Yes, it's okay, our iron horse will just burn a little. Of course, even though we took the car with a fake passport, honestly, we still have to fork out to buy a new car for the leasing company, since it would be better not to leave our DNA here and it would be useful to distract the attention of the security from the gate,' explained Jules.

'Brutal and honest. I would vote for such a candidate,' Henri said patting his brother on the shoulder, and then sitting down with him in the back seat of the car which had just arrived.

'Su, we're in the car. Please write down the address of the gas station at Jiufen, where we are headed for. From there, we'll take a taxi to the airport.' Jules turned to him.

'Well, the second round of the sieve game?' Henri asked enthusiastically.

'Yes, only now the sieve is not armored,' Jules remarked sadly.

'But we're in the back seat. The main thing is to take care of your head. For everything else, I can make you a gorgeous prosthesis.' The elder of the two noted with a smile.

The car moved toward the exit, flying past the knocked-down barrier. Most likely, it demolished the barrier itself, hurrying to meet them. The inability to look through the window was the most difficult in this situation. The brothers sat hunched over in the back seat, trying to be as invisible as possible to prying eyes. A minute, two minutes... Henri seemed to have already heard the loud pounding of his own heart. Waiting is a terrible torment. Very scary. Three minutes... Voices.

'Su, what's the camera showing there?' Henri asked in a whisper.

'Two cars and four men with weapons at the main gate,' Su replied excitedly. 'We're approaching them in sixty seconds; they'll send a request to the car in ten seconds when the car is in their line of sight. So hold on tight; we'll need to race alongside them ASAP. I'll try to aim the car so it doesn't expose you for too long – that way there'll be less chance of them catching you.'

'The alignment is not the most positive.' Henri pointed out categorically.

'Everywhere has its advantages,' said Jules.

'For example?' he asked, grinning.

'The gate has already been broken,' Jules answered cheerfully.

'And you can't argue with that,' Henri agreed.

'Guys, about three seconds,' Su warned them, clutching a small figure of a gilded dragon with pearls in its paws.

'One,' Su began.

'Jules, I wanted to tell you something,' Henri said.

'Two,' Su continued.

'No matter what happens, you can handle everything. I believe in you,' Henri whispered putting his hand on his brother's shoulder, and pressing closer to the back seat.

'I know.'

'Three!' Su shouted, and the car rocketed toward the main exit.

Security got a little confused, but in ten seconds opened fire on the car. The first shots came directly on the windshield, the next ten struck below, punching the front seats of the cabin. The noise sounded eerie. Why? it seemed that the membrane was about to break from the rum, cutting the cannonade.

'How are you?' shouted Henri to his brother.

'Okay. Did it bother you?' he shouted in response.

'No, I'm invulnerable.'

Coming to the last dash, the drone car deftly covered the distance to the gate and, catching up with the guards, set its right side under fire. A series of bullets noisily passed through the right door of the car, after which their Volvo proudly jumped out onto the road, hiding in the darkness of the night.

'Henri?' shouted Jules, brushing shards of glass from the bloody back seat and gently straightening his older brother there.

'Jules, what happened there?' Su shouted anxiously into the phone.

Henri looked at Jules in confusion, carefully examining himself for damage. 'He seems to be intact,' he remarked to himself. 'Only a few deep scratches on his neck.' Carefully running his hand over his brother's forehead,

Henri saw blood there. Strange, because a minute ago, there was nothing there, only if…did this blood belong to Henri himself?

Really? thought the elder brother. 'Yes, you are kidding!' he said aloud, showing Jules his ill-fated left hand on which, in the same place where the little finger was previously hit by a bullet, this time the entire upper phalanx was missing, along with the nail.

'What is it?' Su asked anxiously.

'The upper phalanx of the little finger of his left hand was torn off by a bullet,' Jules whispered, tearing the right sleeve of his shirt to apply a bandage.

'Guys, it's good that in our Chinese version, the red thread of fate is tied to the ankle. If I were Japanese, then my thread would have come off today,' Henri said to the accompaniment of laughter of the guys.

Chapter 7
The Hermit Crab

Translucent, massive, and at the same time weightless, puffs of thick white smoke slowly left the lungs, creating a unique ornate pattern in front of the eyes. After a couple of puffs, the throat became very persistent, which deprived this whole sacred process of its pacifying part. *Well, then,* Jules thought as he put out his cigarette butt, and throwing it into the nearest trashcan, *so I tried what it feels like to smoke.*

It's funny how far those dreams sometimes seem, which we thought of as plans six months ago: courses on playing the ukulele, a workshop for molding articulated dolls, a couple of Spanish lessons, a trip to Japan for the cherry blossom festival next spring... Being realistic, Jules didn't want any of those things. But since they were running out of time, it was probably time for changes.

'Unfortunately, there were no armored models on autopilot as you like, in the rental fleet. Anyway, please come on board,' Henri commanded busily, sitting inside the luxurious Lincoln Continental Mark V in classic black.

'I'm ready,' Jules whispered absently, looking into the distance. 'In which year was this magnificence made?' he asked noticing the car for the first time.

'The magnificence was made in 1986 and the car was made in 1979,' Henri replied contentedly. 'Is that the smell of a Marlboro?' he said getting out of the car. 'I brought you to this land of opportunity, left someone to guard your suitcases for exactly three minutes in the parking lot of the Los Angeles airport, and here you are already starting smoking?' he continued jokingly.

'I decided to thin out the list of "15 things to do before sudden death from a generic curse or a neurochip of unknown origin mounted in the head,"' Jules said fervently, placing an invisible tick on an imaginary list with the index finger of his right hand.

'And how many more points are there in your rating?' his brother asked with interest, as he stowed the suitcases in the trunk.

"Too little for the word rating, but too much for the three remaining days," Jules replied, getting into the car. 'So what's the story with Dr. Laocoon?' he continued fastening his seat belt.

'Zachary... He's a rather straightforward fellow...' Henri replied with a heavy sigh. 'Insanely talented, but too rash and harsh in his statements.'

'How harsh?' Jules asked, rubbing his chin.

'Until the official expulsion from the American Association of Neurosurgeons,' the elder Lero replied, tilting his head and turning the key in the ignition. 'Do you remember my project on individualized smart implants for the cervical spine?' Jules nodded silently. 'He then tried to sabotage us for three years in a row. It seems that no one listened to him, but he ruffled his nerves notably.'

'And what exactly is known about his expulsion from the association? The reason must be very serious.'

'In short, a series of rather famous articles with a slightly racist and gender chauvinistic connotation, followed by several equally resounding interviews. I don't think he is an ardent sexist or racist, he is most likely just prone to rather harsh conclusions, contrary to the common sense of most healthy people. This is a widespread phenomenon among professionals who have succeeded in a particular narrow field. Like all people, they are lazy by nature and, not wanting to waste time studying the processes and phenomena occurring in other areas of knowledge, they simply apply their previous experience to everything that they see, naturally considering themselves a competent expert in absolutely foreign fields... Such people do not need condemnation, but sympathy and enlightenment. You know how greedy modern society has become for public online executions. Many thousands of years have passed and people are still in anticipation of a careless gesture or word to persecute someone. As if there was no Savior and his Sacrifice, as if we are all that part of humanity that did not survive the Great Flood. We are all that part of humanity that remained underwater, that part that still lives in the Old Testament.'

'Like a fish,' Jules added, absentmindedly looking into the distance.

"Fish..." Henri agreed. 'Now he is a loner, having abandoned almost all of his previous connections and developments.'

'Cancer hermit?' Jules remarked with a smile.

'Hermit crab,' Henri confirmed, nodding.

It took about half an hour to get to the bottom of Santa Monica Boulevard, after which they were safely in West Hollywood.

'I assume this is the center of the local Russian community?' asked Jules incredulously, looking back at the signs in an incomprehensible language.

'Yes, he moved here five years ago. This is a very good place for an introvert. If you are not particularly smiling, then you can pass for a local,' Henri answered, frowning. 'I would fit well here. Mysterious and with an eternal craving for self-examination. Do I remind you of Dostoevsky's hero?'

'No, Henri. Let's start with your unrestrained friendliness, especially toward the opposite sex,' Jules jokingly remarked, immediately receiving a push in the side.

Having parked the car next to a small residential building, the guys moved in the direction of Zachary's apartment taking with them two small suitcases. The apartment was located just above a small coffee shop around the corner. Walking around the main entrance of the establishment, they came to an ornate iron staircase at the end of the building. Climbing up to the second floor, they came close to a metal door above which a couple of cameras hung.

'Mister Laocoon,' Jules said, pressing the video call at the front door. 'We'd like to talk to you. I am Jules Lero from the Paris-based Lero-Group.'

After a few minutes of silence, the door slowly opened and a very tall and sturdy man appeared in front of them, who looked about forty or forty-five years old. He was dressed in rumpled gray checked home trousers with stretched knees and a dark blue T-shirt with the inscription "Andromeda" emblazoned on it. The ensemble was completed with dark green Converse sneakers, torn at the sides, which, together with a heavily neglected beard, gave the man an impressive resemblance to a homeless person.

'Zachary, we haven't seen each other for so long,' Henri said, smiling impeccably.

Hearing such a greeting, the man looked from Jules standing opposite him to a satisfied Henri and at the same second closed the door in front of them.

'You say you once "quarreled a little?"' Jules specified, raising his left eyebrow skeptically.

'Just a little verbal skirmish. Well… And a couple of drunken fights. Quite tiny,' the brunette justified himself, shrugging his shoulders, coming closer to the video call.

'Zachary, well, don't be such a bitch. We come in peace, honestly. I'm here with my little brother, we need to get the neurochip out of his head. Let us come in, I'll explain everything.'

'Get out!' Doctor Laocoon threw at them from the door.

'So what now?' Jules whispered in confusion.

'We use the trump card,' Henri replied in French. 'I have a sample,' he shouted into the camera, switching back to English and showing the suitcase he had brought.

The door opened at the same moment and, leaning his shoulder on the doorframe, the doctor, looking at the floor and in a low voice, commanded, 'Come on in.'

Putting the teacups on a low glass table, he immediately began to examine the neurochip they had brought.

'Some kind of madness…' he whispered barely audibly. 'I warned that it will be so…' angrily looking at Henri, he said louder.

'Yes, you turned out to be right, everything led to this…' Henri agreed guiltily dropping his eyes, handing him a folder with Jules's MRI scans.

Slowly turning the pages, the doctor turned his gaze to the youngest of the brothers.

'I believe that since you are here, this is a very delicate matter and most likely urgent,' he concluded.

'Right. You need to start today,' Jules answered without blinking.

'Well… I need about an hour to check, but I'm ninety percent sure that we will get by with stereotaxic radiosurgery. Simply put, we will disable the chip by non-contact radiation, without trepanation and anesthesia. The branches from the main part are too skillfully implanted, so we will not touch them. I honestly don't understand at all how this was possible, so we'd better leave them as they are. We will carry out the operation at midnight today. I will agree with the operating room and the staff for you, of course, to pay the rent and this is the fee,' he whispered, writing a rather large amount on the back of the prints with pictures.

'Well. That's all?' Henri said, getting up and stretching out his hand to seal the deal.

The doctor thought for a moment, and a second later, he gave Henri a fierce hook to the left.

'Now, yes,' he added.

Henri nodded silently, and the guys finally sealed the deal with a handshake.

Going down the spiral staircase to the car, Jules patted his brother on the shoulder sympathetically.

'By the end of our trip, I will have turned into Frankenstein,' Henri said fervently, rubbing his aching jaw with his right hand, and showing his brother the severed left little finger.

'It will only make you even more mysterious,' Jules remarked, opening the salon door.

'You know, it's ironic that I always thought my father was more conservative on most issues than my uncle. To be honest, I was just inhumanly surprised to learn that of the two, it was the father who lived on the yacht.' Henri grinned.

'Our father is a sea wolf and our uncle is an exemplary family man with two children. We knew so little about them,' Jules agreed as he fastened his seat belt.

'It's about half an hour's drive to our uncle's house. After the tragedy, his family left for Oregon to stay with relatives, so we can safely search the house for any clues. I suggest that you first stop at one of the fish restaurants in Santa Monica, then take a shower and change at some hotel nearby, and when it gets dark, move toward the house.'

'Another break-in with penetration into a foreign country.' Jules noted with a heavy sigh. 'But even in such circumstances, it's nice to know that we are cosmopolitan.'

After their supper and preparations were finished, the brothers finally moved toward Uncle Jacques's house.

'This is one of the nastiest pairs of shoes that have ever been on my beautiful feet.' Henri had been grumbling for the last ten minutes, looking suspiciously at the safety shoes on his feet prepared by his younger brother.

'Don't complain. These are classic combat boots. By the way, I'm still wondering why Laocoon agreed to help us?' Jules said as he turned off the highway.

'He's strange, crazy, stubborn, but above all, he's a doctor. A real doctor who took the Hippocratic Oath. The model was just baited, and the reward was just a means to keep them going. It's just that this is the way of ideological people, people for whom vows mean something,' Henri concluded, pulling on the hood of his baseball cap.

'Thomas was such a person…' Jules whispered with a smile.

'Sometimes it's hard for me to believe that he was a real person,' Henri agreed with sadness, looking somewhere into the distance.

Then the brothers continued their journey in silence, each immersed in their memories until the silence was interrupted by the noise of a passing car.

'Here we'd better turn off, so as not to shine a light, there are still many private houses in the vicinity. I'll walk out here a bit and try to get into the house from the backyard. For now, park nearby and wait for my call. Perhaps the police or other intruders are in the house,' Henri suggested, putting on a pair of leather gloves.

'Okay, take care of your little finger,' Jules replied, patting the elder on the shoulder with a smile.

The house in which their uncle spent the last years of his life was located on a small hillock, away from the rest of the neighbors. Henri climbed up from the road for about five minutes, finding himself directly opposite the main gate. The wall separating the house from the outside world was concrete and high enough to see the windows on the first floor, plus it was already dark enough outside.

Looking around, he walked to the backyard. As they could see from satellite maps, there were several rather large ficus trees growing at the back of the fence. Trying not to use the crippled little finger, Henri quite deftly climbed up and in a minute jumped over the fence, successfully landing on the soft grass.

The courtyard was quite large. On its left side, there was an open gazebo rising from behind the bushes and a small pool a little closer to the house. To Henri's right hand, there were several swings, a small fountain neatly framed with flowers, and a cute treehouse directly opposite the cottage.

Henri was already walking forward in the direction of one of the rear doors, but suddenly he heard an extraneous rustle, apparently coming from behind the bushes right behind the gazebo on the left. Trying not to move, he waited for the situation to develop in the hope that the rustle was due to his overly rich imagination, or just a breath of wind. Unfortunately, the rustle didn't even think to shut up. Increasingly, it turned into the sound of someone's heavy footsteps, and a few moments later two black silhouettes appeared in front of the bushes.

Henri swallowed nervously. Dusk had already receded by that hour, and in the oncoming night, the courtyard was illuminated only by the moonlight and a lone dim lantern located in the left corner of the courtyard. The lantern illuminated only a small part of the left half of the courtyard, making it almost impossible to see the strangers. Judging by their outlines, they were quite small. Could it be children? *Stop!* thought Henri. *My uncle has two children. Didn't they go to Oregon to stay with relatives?*

'Guys,' Henri began taking off his hood. 'Sorry, I didn't mean to scare you at all. My name is Henri, I am your...' He didn't manage to finish the phrase.

Hearing his greeting, two small silhouettes moved in the direction of his voice, and a few minutes later two giant Newfoundlands emerged from the lantern. Each of them was about eighty centimeters high and the dimensions reminded him of brown bears. But the most frightening thing was not the size of this couple. The worst thing was to see their eyes seething with anger, eyes red with anger.

'Okay...' Henri whispered. 'Take it easy. These are Newfoundlands. These dogs and flies will not offend; they cannot because of their nature. They do not have hunting instincts at the genetic level, since they are hereditary rescuers. This breed does not even bark,' he finished under a lingering deafening roar, from the distant dogs, exposing their impressive incisors, and foaming at the mouth.

It took Henri only a second to assess the situation. The most suitable option for him now was only a treehouse. With a jerk, he sprinted, overcoming the cherished thirty meters, nervously shifting his legs, and climbed up the small perches nailed to the tree trunk as the sounds of clinking fangs came from below.

Leaping inside, Henri looked around. There was a small table in the corner, a couple of empty shelves that had probably held toys, and an old checkered blanket. The body of the house was strong, so it was not possible to tear off a piece in the form of a stick with a nail. There was a window on the right wall of the house, just at the level of one of the windows of the house, on the second floor. The only problem was that they were separated by about five meters and with all the will in the world, he could hardly have jumped there. Looking down, Henri saw that the dogs were still hanging around the tree house and, jumping quite high, trying to reach it.

'Not a bad try, guys, but before you succeed, you still need to jump at least four meters higher,' he quipped, referring to his new friends.

And as soon as he grimaced in a satisfied grin, one of the dogs, as if understanding what he was talking about, got up on his hind legs and, leaning his forepaws on a tree trunk, seemed as if he had created himself...a springboard for his comrade's jumping.

'Well, no...' Henri whispered, shaking his head skeptically. 'Of course, something is wrong with them, but... They are not going to...'

At the same moment, the second dog, running away, and then jumping on his hind legs on the back of its comrade, it could reach most of the way, but then fell to the ground in failure. Yes, he had only one and a half meters of success.

'This is some kind of madness,' whispered Henri, disbelieving what he had seen.

Having run even further, the dog ran with all his might and, having made a new jump, almost caught up with the upper perch of the wooden staircase. At the same second, Henri, not being at a loss, decided to stop the dog's subsequent attempts to climb, hitting him hard in the face with an army boot. Having fallen, the dog issued a lingering roar and began to gnaw the lower perch of the ladder, trying to tear it away from the tree. Taking a breath, Henri decided to warn his brother about the danger.

'Well, finally,' Jules replied. 'I thought that you had something wrong with the little finger again.'

'Jules, stay outside for now. There are a couple of evil as hell Newfoundlands here who drove me into the treehouse in the backyard. I don't understand how to enter the house yet,' Henri blurted out in a hurry.

'Newfoundlands?' the younger man repeated incredulously. 'This is one of the friendliest dog breeds in the world; by definition, they cannot be aggressive.'

'I know it sounds crazy,' Henri agreed, looking down at the dog jumping up at the tree. 'I suppose that they're someone...' Looking closely, he realized that he did not see where the second dog had disappeared to. 'Stop... There was still…' Before he could finish, Henri turned to the sound of breaking glass and saw a huge dog's mouth flying at him from the window of the second floor.

In a second, the dog overcame the distance separating them and with a drawn-out roar flew into the window of the tree house, simultaneously knocking Henri down. Having dropped the phone, he managed to crawl aside, hitting the dog a couple of times in the face with the same boot. During the third attempt, the dog in the most unsuccessful way intercepted his right leg by the boot, trying to bite through the thick skin. Henri decided to free his foot from the boot, holding the sole by force and at the same time pushing the animal away from him with his free left foot.

It only took him a few times to look into the dog's eyes to make sure that they no longer belonged to the dog. They were eyes demanding blood, the eyes of the beast. Finally enraged, the creature firmly grabbed Henri's left leg with its claws, piercing it just above the knee. Henri slowly turned his eyes to the wound and then to the beast and, with a jerk, pushed the shoe in his hands deep into the animal's throat, trying to take his right hand out of the dog as quickly as possible. The creature retreated from him into a corner and, in an unsuccessful attempt to free itself from a deeply stuck shoe, convulsively swallowed air, and after a couple of minutes fell on its side unconscious. Catching his breath, Henri grabbed the phone lying next to him.

'Jules? Things are good. There is only one dog left.'

'Oh… I know.' He heard both from the phone and also from somewhere below. Approaching the stairs, he saw Jules standing below in a baseball cap, with a chisel in his hands. 'This demon heard me when I opened the gate. Miraculously, I managed to close it in the garage at the entrance,' Jules said, and after a little hesitation, added, 'they…'

'Most likely with neurochips.' Henri finished climbing down the steps.

'Are you okay?' examining him, the younger brother asked.

'He bit my left leg. Are you uninjured?' asked Henri and, after waiting for his mute nod, invited him to enter the house.

The panoramic windows of the first floor overlooking the courtyard were surprisingly open. The fairly spacious living room directly opposite the entrance had a lounge area with a low square table in black beech and a cute ivory sofa framing it. Opposite the sofa was a large bookcase with an endless number of bookshelves. Coming closer, Henri noticed that the volumes were arranged by authors in alphabetical order, which was characteristic of their father, but certainly not his uncle. Although... We do not know ourselves, so how can we judge others?

'Look at these sweethearts.' Showing his brother the family photo found on the coffee table with his uncle, his wife, and two adorable babies of nine and seven years old, Jules was touched. 'Our cousins.'

'Girls...' Henri drawled thoughtfully. 'You know, they say that intelligence at the genetic level is inherited only by daughters.'

'And then what is passed on to the sons?' the younger asked, raising his eyebrows in surprise.

'Development of the limbic system, in other words, a typical emotional state,' answered Henri passing further into the bar area.

'Oh...my poor nephews,' Jules commented sarcastically, putting the photo back on the coffee table.

'As an elder, I will again make a wise face with the expression "I didn't hear that."' Henri smiled slyly, pouring an uncorked bottle of vintage cognac of the family reserve from 1960 into small stemless glasses. Jules and Thomas loved to call their tumblers when they were kids. 'You do the office and I'll check the bedroom.'

'1960...' gently accepting the outstretched glass, Jules quietly whispered, slowly inhaling the aroma. 'The year of the collapse of the colonial system and most of the state colonies in Africa gaining independence.'

'For such a luxurious drink, tubular glasses would be more suitable, but I remember too well how you loved such tumblers,' Henri said as he approached his brother.

'For Jacques and Albert Lero, who will be with us forever. No matter how many times they die,' Jules said with a sad smile.

'Always,' Henri whispered after draining his glass.

'Well, shall we go?' Jules asked Henri, nodding toward the stairs.

'Run ahead while I wash away the remnants of our DNA,' taking the empty glass from his brother, Henri muttered with a smile.

As he approached the sink, Henri heard Jules's footsteps as he climbed the stairs. *What were they? Their lives,* he thought as he turned the valve on the tap. 'Father's depression after the death of our mother, when he refused to leave the office for months. Smiling, but always exhausted and always lonely uncle. Sometimes to start living, you need to die once.'

After drying the carefully washed glasses, Henri slowly walked toward the bedroom, nodding along the way to Jules, who was busy looking in the study.

The bedroom of his uncle and his wife was located at the end of the second-floor corridor. The room was quite spacious and consisted of the main room, bathroom, and dressing room. Approaching a large oak bed with carved legs, Henri carefully examined the contents of the surface of the bedside tables and then boldly went to the more ascetic of them. Opening the first drawer, he found a pair of working notebooks and several books on shipping and meteorology inside. He looked into the second drawer and Henri's heart skipped a beat… At the bottom was a blue-black laptop.

'So…' Henri whispered, gently pressing the power button. *And now the magic will begin. Let's take something simple,* he thought, sorting through flash drives in his pocket. 'What about Cain and Abel?' he whispered interrogatively, nodding to the laptop. 'Excellent choice, sir,' Henri replied in a low voice to himself, inserting the USB stick.

Running the program, he slowly looked at his watch. Half-past nine… Very soon for the operation… Putting his hand back in his pocket, he felt there that very figure from the anime, left for him by Thomas. This gesture has become his evening ceremony to calm the nerves.

'If only I…' Had time to rush through his head, but his thoughts were interrupted by a vibrating phone. Pulling it carefully from his trouser pocket, Henri stared at the screen in disbelief.

'Unknown number? On a disposable SIM card of a disposable phone? Really?' Henri carefully put the phone on the bed and stared at the monitor, leafing through open files.

'So, what do we have here… Working papers, family photos…' he whispered slowly while the phone continued to vibrate, destroying the silence surrounding him.

'More photos, videos from children's parties, work reports and… Oh… A couple of hidden password-protected archives. Now we'll pick up the code,' having put the folder on hacking, he muttered contentedly, still looking back at the ringing phone.

'I'm listening,' he said in English, but he couldn't stand it and picked up the phone.

'I see you don't miss me at all,' a woman's voice said sternly in French.

'Aunt Selena…' Henri began cautiously. 'As on time, though… I would have liked to have heard from you earlier. Much earlier!' he answered in an icy tone, switching to bass.

'How do you like the latest news about our Taiwan branch?' she asked evenly.

'I haven't had the pleasure of hearing anything yet. Maybe you will be the one to finally open my eyes and ears?' he continued forcefully.

'I heard that it is raining in Paris now and it is so dangerous for you to catch a cold. I'm worried about you, Henri. Jules seems to be immune to any infection, but you can get very sick. You'd better go home,' suggested his aunt, making her voice a little higher.

'Well, how can a groomsman leave the groom alone?' he replied, feigning misunderstanding.

'So take Jules with you. Marriage is not water, somehow he will live without it,' the aunt insistently suggested, immediately adding, 'I will book your seats on a charter flight tonight, tomorrow night you will already be in Hong Kong. This is the best option for both of you.'

Henri shifted his gaze from the window to the monitor screen and did not breathe looking at the contents of the opened archive. Sometimes it is difficult to believe our own eyes if they show something that we do not want to see.

'It's not just about the two of us anymore. It's about something much bigger than both of us,' Henri whispered, hanging up and staring in horror at the monitor where thousands of files with more than four hundred varieties of "sea angels" neurochips flashed in front of him.

****

'I definitely can't stay?' once again, Henri asked Dr. Zachary Laocoon, with hope in his voice, glancing at Jules chatting with the nurse.

'I told you…' Zachary repeated, exhaling heavily. 'We'll set everything up, for now, select the right wave, plus the procedure itself. Altogether, it'll take no more than an hour. You will only get in the way and distract him too much.'

'Yes, Henri washed your leg for now.' The younger brother waved to him from behind.

'Your voice is too pleased to be the patient to be operated on,' Henri remarked sarcastically.

'I'm still glad that the hair will not suffer. Non-invasive surgery is wonderful,' Jules replied, showing his thumb, and beaming with happiness.

'Here are the keys to the shower,' Zachary said, holding out the bundle. 'Wash your leg when you're done, we'll give you an injection just in case. Oh, and let's see the little finger,' with curiosity, looking at the bandaged finger, he whispered. 'What have you got there?'

'I'll show you when I return. Let the intrigue hang in the air for now,' the elder Lero replied with a sly smile, jokingly raising his right eyebrow.

'Yes…' Zachary managed skeptically. 'I'm all excited,' he added, pointing to the door.

Henri once again waved to Jules and slowly trudged down the dark corridor toward the elevator.

The hospital was empty, and if not for his recent adventures in Seoul, he would likely have found a certain charm in it. Reaching the shower room, Henri slowly pulled off his clothes, trying not to think about the ongoing operation. There was nothing dangerous for his brother's life in here, and he would not have been able to help in anything and really would only have interfered. He needed to calm down. Standing under the shower built into the ceiling, Henri, shuddering from the cold, slowly turned the valve.

'Interesting,' he mused. 'Can that part of you, which you first of all try to warm under a hot shower, be considered the most probable location of the "cradle of your soul?"'

Hot drops flowing down his collarbones continued their long journey, skirting the stomach, hips, and knees of their route, inevitably striving for the enchanting, but at the same time insanely sad repose of their short, but certainly bright path. All of them ended up beautifully shattered on the bottom of slightly cracked tiles, which most likely survived their best times back in the middle of the last century.

Despite being as vintage as the tiles themselves, the shower had been running for about ten minutes, and the room has just begun to fill with steam.

I need to fix the broken holder in my shower, he thought, recalling his apartment in Guangzhou. 'It's funny how strange and at the same time simple our world is arranged. It is only when you are twelve that your bathroom will be warm, it will be tolerable, and most likely not with a broken holder… In adulthood, most things will relentlessly remind you of your sins. Each of us did not complete something, forgot something, did not undertake something. Each of us has our own broken holder in the bathroom, reminding us of the imperfection of ourselves and the perfection of our parents. Parents…' Henri took another deep breath.

Of course, there were many scenarios with that data on my uncle's computer. Among the obvious ones either the collection of information about a possible threat or the consolidation of information about a tactical advantage came to mind. Now it was necessary to use all kinds of resources and try to consider all the options.

The phone in the right corner of the room vibrated loudly. Quickly grabbing a towel, Henri checked the smartphone in which he found a message from Laocoon.

'We managed rather quickly. The patient is doing well. Come quickly for an injection before the foam comes out of your mouth. P. S. I want to sleep, so come here ASAP!'

Sighing with relief, Henri quickly put on his trousers and threw a sweatshirt over his naked body, grabbed a T-shirt of linen, and ran barefoot out of the shower. Only when he got to the elevator did he realize that such a rush was, most likely, unnecessary.

'We did it,' he whispered as he pressed the elevator button. 'We are finally free. There is no and never was any damn curse. To hell with it all, to hell with Paris, let's just run away somewhere to the Philippines or New Zealand!'

The elevator stopped, in the opening door in front of him stood a serious and very alarmed Jules.

'I remembered something, Henri,' he whispered. 'A lot of everything. We have a lot to talk about it.'

Chapter 8
Fishes

The autumn Parisian sun had long gone beyond the horizon when Henri was finishing his walk through the cozy and deserted Parisian streets. The tourist season was behind and the cold weather was still quite far away, which made this time ideal for leisurely hiking trails. Conveniently dangling his legs from a small pier, almost opposite the gracefully towering towers of the main building of the French National Library, he enjoyed watching the boats passing by, a couple of which were floating bars.

'More floating or bars?' He went through the options with interest in his head. 'Technically, the facility is still in operation and is still formally performing its transport and river functions, although to be honest, the proud word "ship" does not fit here at all.'

The ship... Henri's thoughts instantly went into the era of great geographical discoveries. Eternal search, risk, excitement... People went to sea to meet the unknown, to know the limit, to find the end of their path or just the end of this world. Nowadays, such travels are more likely to be reduced to functional routes for transporting goods, guarding borders, or fishing. Gone is that invisible but incredibly exciting element of the search for truth, from which the blood runs cold in the veins and the heart sinks. The element that generates the only feeling in this world capable of overshadowing all fears and instincts of human nature without exception. The feeling that, like a wild beast, sits somewhere deep inside, waiting for its hour and capable of instantly tearing apart even the most ancient and uterine instinct of a person – the instinct of self-preservation, stronger than which it is difficult to find. This is that almighty beast whose name is curiosity.

Here you have a piece of greed and a lion's share of pride, a little envy, a lot of intellectual gluttony, a lot of anger, and even more despondency from the lack of an opportunity to satisfy your insatiable desire to know. Desire, which is essentially a form of mental lust. All seven deadly sins in one bottle called "curiosity." The curiosity behind which Henri would no doubt rush into the wildest and most dangerous adventure on a spaceship somewhere to the other end of the universe. Just somewhere to infinity. 'What is there?' raising his head to the night sky, he whispered with a deep sigh.

'No white gold inserts, no diamond buttons. Only a laconic black European suit, most likely from a mixture of cashmere and silk. A thin white stripe on the lapels of a jacket on both sides, a white silk shirt, an emerald-colored tie in a black cage with a small copper clip… Modesty suits you, Monsieur Leroy.' Jules, dressed in a white tailcoat, turned to him with a dazzling smile, holding out a glass of hot latte to his brother…

'Today you are not only behaving, but you also look like an angel,' Henri replied, pointing to his snow-white suit.

'I'm trying to keep the brand, but I'm sorry I won't sit next to you. The marina looks rather dirty. I parked in a paid parking lot around the corner, so we can sit here for a while and drive slowly to the Richelieu building.'

'I still cannot believe that your chosen one managed to rent that very Oval Hall of the National Library, designed by Jean-Louis Pascal at the end of the nineteenth century.' Henri was surprised.

'And I still don't believe that we are going to do what we are planning tonight,' the younger man whispered anxiously looking at the ship sailing past, sipping with pleasure the vanilla cappuccino he had reserved for himself.

'Did you take everything? Were there any problems?' turning his head toward him, Henri asked.

'Yes, Lu Su and I phoned and checked again on the way here. Just as you said,' Jules reassured him, patting his brother on the shoulder.

'Well, then I'll suggest a coffee toast. Let's drink to beautiful Paris and all the beautiful cities of this planet, and may one day we'll boldly be able to call all this home without stupid divisions into cities, peoples, and countries. For a wonderful, wondrous place called "planet Earth,"' he finished, and clinking glasses with his younger brother in an orderly manner, he got to his feet.

'I, as always, do not quite catch the connection, but who cares. To the dregs!' Nodded Jules, with sarcasm, victoriously finishing his cappuccino.

'The navigator writes about a twelve-minute drive, so taking into account the traffic jams, we will be there just in time for the cocktails.' Henri threw in a businesslike step forward.

'Why should we rush to the time of serving cocktails? Did you ask to mix Thomas's Fall of Zion?' suggested Jules, still standing on the pier.

'Made a couple of calls from Seoul airport. I'm your groomsman, after all.' Jules didn't elaborate, but he understood perfectly well that even in the darkest time Henri did not disown Thomas. Even then in Seoul, when everything around it ceased to seem normal.

'Do you want to drive?' taking out the keys, the younger of the brothers, who was approaching the car, suggested.

'No, now is your time.' He nodded in response and the brothers hit the road again.

The views of Paris at night, as always, awakened a string of vivid memories in Henri. The first trip to the Vienna Woods, the first ballet at the Opera Garnier and... Oh, even the first kiss by the Canal Saint-Martin, he noted to himself dreamily rolling his eyes. Night, guitar, and a bottle of red wine.

The closer they got to their destination, the easier and brighter the pictures from the long-forgotten past appeared before him. Interestingly, he didn't think about it for decades, but the funniest thing is that to refresh these images in his mind, it took him only a few seconds. A few seconds to look over his whole life.

'We'll park here, I don't want to look for the car among the endless number of iron horses of my wedding guests,' Jules commented, nodding toward the resulting traffic jams.

'Later? I see you are optimistic,' Henri said, opening the door.

'Well, formally this is a wedding, not a commemoration.' Jules winked back as he got out of the car.

The sounds of a waltz playing in the garden spread over several blocks around.

'"Autumn Dream" by Archibald Joyce? An excellent choice, Henri,' Jules praised his older brother, entering the garden where cocktails were already being served with might and main.

'I agree, the choice is fine, but not mine,' he confirmed, looking absentmindedly around.

There were already about a hundred guests in the garden alone. The phrase "closest people" has undergone semantic changes over the past 19 years that he was absent from the capital. The guests enjoyed the reception, a good part of them lined up for personal congratulations from the groom. Jules politely accepted the wishes of long and happy family life, going to the fountain opposite the entrance to the library to remain in his brother's field of vision. That evening they could not separate in any way.

'Was Monsieur Leroy just too busy the last weeks or did he grow bangs on purpose? It evokes memories,' a deep female voice sounded behind him, from which it was as if thousands of small needles were thrust into Henri's shoulder. He did not need to turn around to understand who was now behind him.

'It evokes,' slowly sipping from the glass, he answered without moving, so as not to lose sight of Jules. 'Like this waltz. "Autumn forest," isn't it? I remember that you hated him a lot and even wanted to break your finger or drown the piano in a pond, just so as not to play it at the graduation concert.'

'Surprising,' almost touching his shoulder blades, the speaker whispered somewhere in the area of his head. 'I never thought that Monsieur Leroy remembers at least something that does not concern his person.' An icy voice seemed to walk over his body, awakening in him the memories of the very night when he found the lifeless body of Marie-Julie in her bedroom… Henri looked at his brother, then dropped his gaze into his glass, trying to concentrate on the waltz to somehow calm himself down.

'Not at all,' he admitted, barely breathing. 'I remember quite a lot. For example, your brother was a very good pianist. Will he play for us today? Well, in honor of a long separation?' he whispered watching her through the reflection in the glass.

'Will he play? Unless, your brother plays for us,' she replied with a laugh, slightly tilting her head to his face. 'You're still funny…' Passing her left hand over his bangs, Marie-Julie whispered, adding a little later: I hope you will give me at least one dance today, my emo-boy.

Henri felt her slowly remove her chin from his shoulder and silently walk away somewhere to the side.

Well, Perseus, he thought, rubbing the bridge of his nose, and draining his glass. *We managed to avoid the direct gaze of the jellyfish.*

The celebration was just beginning to gain momentum when the guests were invited to enter the main hall for the ceremony – the famous and incomparable Oval Hall of the National French Library. The organizers of the celebration managed to persuade the local administration to temporarily move all the reading tables and information racks, freeing up the main area of the hall to install a rather massive stage, a dance area in the center, where the main part of the event and tables for guests around the perimeter would be held.

Giant bookcases wrapped around the hall from all sides and the crown of this masterpiece, in addition to the priceless publications collected there, was an incredibly beautiful oval-shaped glass dome in the center of the room and about twenty hatches framing it along the edges. The color of the decorations used in the decoration of the room was matched to the main scale of the hall, and even in the invitation cards for the guests, the presence of an emerald green garment was a necessary item of the dress code.

Looking around at the figures of the guests, Henri mentally counted almost forty representatives of their Trust, plus about a dozen famous politicians. There were about the same number of high-ranking socialites and half a dozen famous businessmen, among whom there were more than twenty representatives of companies researching the field of neuroprosthetics. About forty remaining people were completely unknown to Henri, which altogether worried him greatly. They were unlikely to be anybody's relatives, he thought nervously.

'Ladies and gentlemen, we ask everyone to go to the reception area to open tonight with the ceremony of the merger of the East End Investment Company and the Octava Trust Fund,' the presenter of the ceremony said from the stage, gesturing to the central part of the hall, where guests had already begun to flock. Following the example of the crowd, Henri walked slowly toward the center of the room. Despite the hum around, he could hear the heavy raindrops clattering on the glass roof of the dome above his head.

'Monsieur Leroy, do you think the dome is strong enough? The rain seems to be gaining such momentum that very soon it will turn into a real downpour.' A tall man dressed in a dark brown suit with a dark green brooch in the form of an oak leaf, clutching a glass of champagne, turned to him.

'Depends on the nature of the shower. I hope that this is not a flood, Monsieur Oak,' Henri answered politely shaking his hand, unable to hold back a smile, because whatever you say, and the representatives of the Oak family were always famous for their practicality and foresight, which made them very close to the Cigogny house, whose head was now drinking a Mount Fuji cocktail. She was now talking to the heads of the families of the Needles, Castors and Langlais at the opposite end of the room.

Marie-Julie Langlaist, as the true head of the house, could not appear at the reception without the family brooch in the form of a scarlet rose proudly flaunted on her amazing emerald dress with a high collar and an elegant neckline at the back. The shade of Mademoiselle Langlaist's lipstick, like the shoes, was meticulously matched to the tone of the brooch. She listened attentively to her interlocutors, often straightening the luxurious mane of her curly hair, neatly styled on the right side. Chuck Aigle, standing on her right hand, nodded his head all the time – the girl aroused heightened interest in him, which, in principle, he did not hide by actively gesturing and touching her in conversation.

Louis Cartier, who was next to him, was peacefully drinking the Caesar cocktail, but was not very verbose, however, as he had been during his studies at the boarding school. The young man was a distant relative of them. In his first years of study, Henri took over the mentorship of the youngster to look after him, but Louis got tired of such tutelage pretty quickly and their friendship faded by itself.

'The weather can be quite unpredictable at times,' Henri added, returning to the dialogue.

'The weather in unpredictability is still very, very far from people,' a short gray-haired man who looked about sixty-five or seventy years old intervened with a smile.

'Monsieur Loup.' Stretching out his hand for a handshake, Henri turned to him involuntarily looking at the cufflinks of the man made in the form of an elegant flower. 'Are they dahlias?' he clarified.

'Daisies. And on your cufflinks today…' Loup looked interestedly at Henri's cufflinks. 'Hmm… Is that a perch?'

'No. This is not a specific one, just a fish. I didn't wear something especially bright today, I was afraid to unwittingly outshine the groom,' he joked, rubbing his wrist. 'By the way, Jules today put on the family cufflinks that belonged to our father, the ones with the rooster.'

'I remember them,' agreed Monsieur Loup, nodding his head approvingly. 'Your father wore them to every official event. It's very delicate work.'

'Dear guests, we invite the hosts of this evening to the stage for a welcoming speech and a solemn ceremony of signing an agreement on the merger of organizations,' the host announced with a smile. 'Please welcome Mademoiselle Mila Nicole Crule, CEO of the East End Investment Company, and Monsieur Jules Emmanuel Lero, head of the Octave Trust.'

To the cheers of two hundred gathered guests, Jules took Mademoiselle Crule by the arm and went up to the stage. The whiteness of their carefully matched outfits was diluted only by the emerald neckerchief of the groom and the light green ornament on the bride's belt. Mila, being a very tall girl in herself, today seemed almost the same height as Jules, if not a couple of centimeters taller. High heels, straight-cut trousers, a long satin train running from the beltline. The whole set, together with a well-chosen high hairstyle, made her visually twenty to twenty-five centimeters taller.

Finally, having approached the ceremonial place of the signing of the contract, Mademoiselle Koulet, manly correcting a strand of hair that had strayed from her perfect hair, sealed the contract with her signature, of course, after making sure that Monsieur Leroy did the same.

'It's done!' the presenter announced in a festive tone to the applause of the audience and the solemn handshake of the signers. 'The era of our cooperation has finally come!'

'Sure...' Monsieur Loup whispered skeptically, nodding his head. 'But only if the past joint machinations with the participation of most of today's guests do not count at all.'

'I have no idea what you are talking about.' Monsieur Oak, who was standing next to him, looked at him menacingly.

'Nothing has essentially changed and will never change. In history, everything is always cyclical,' Loup continued, reluctantly clapping with everyone in the audience.

'Did you manage to personally find all the existing epochs to check it?' Henri asked him ironically, raising his left eyebrow pointedly.

'Well, I have a Ph.D. in mathematics. I don't need to check what I already know, because these are facts,' Loup replied with a wide smile.

'But I would not be in a hurry with conclusions. After all, even if we take for the truth everything that, having passed through an innumerable number of prisms of someone else's subjectivity, is presented to us as the past and the present that we have, but the future is still unknown to anyone, and maybe life can still make a very unexpected somersault that will greatly surprise us...

More than that, lately I have concluded that you need to trust, not the facts, but you need to trust people,' Henri said with a smile.

'Oh, this is all very nice, of course,' retorted Monsieur Loup, laughing, as he patted Henri on the shoulder, and headed to the banquet area.

The nicest thing, the eldest of Lero's sons thought, grinning, is that none of my acquaintances in the humanities talks about his doctorate as often and indiscriminately concerning the subject of communication as their colleagues with degrees in the exact sciences.

'Gentlemen, now that the official part of the event is over, we are waiting for a festive auction and a solemn wedding ceremony that will close the evening. The auction will begin in ten minutes, please take your seats at the banquet tables,' the host announced, beaming like a brand new franc, and leaving the stage to general applause as gave a sign to the musicians who were already leaving.

'Monsieur Oak,' Monsieur Aigle, who came up to them, began with a charming smile, 'I'm sure there's a gorgeous bonsai that deserves your attention at today's auction like nothing else,' he concluded with a friendly pat on the back for Oak, who didn't show his emotions, as always.

'Chuck, buddy, the evening has just begun and I see you are already telling others with might and main what they should do?' gave out Oberon, who was approaching the audience, theatrically raising his palms and slightly shaking his head, in the company of the only one with whom he somehow got along in the Trust – Daniel Drago.

'Oberon, buddy, how glad I am that you survived the fire,' Chuck muttered through clenched teeth, still holding a smile on his face, but already loosening its tension by about one and a half centimeters.

'How could I end our eternal friendship in such a sad way? You and I will always be together, buddy. Until the very end,' Oberon answered cheerfully, drinking his Moscow mule contentedly.

'I can't wait for this end,' Chuck drawled, weakening the smile still smoldering on his face by another half a centimeter.

'Dear guests' – the presenter from the stage again turned to those present – 'we ask you to take your places at the banquet tables. The auction will start in two minutes. All officially registered bidders can find the bidding boards prepared for them near the designated locations.'

Banquet tables were located along the perimeter of the entire hall on the right and left sides of the stage. The tables, like the hall itself, had an oval shape and could accommodate up to fourteen people. However, to free an overview of the central part of the room, where, as Henri understood from the words of Monsieur Loup, the lots of today's auction would be displayed for everyone to see, the guests were seated only from the outside of the tables, filling the tables by half. In total, he counted twenty-eight tables with seven guests along the perimeter of the hall and one central table right next to the stage. Henri sat down in the place prepared for him, two tables clockwise from the center table, where Jules sat with Mademoiselle Crule and five other members of the board of directors of the East End Investment Company.

As expected, Henri did not find any plaques next to his name, as did all the guests sitting at his table. The owners of the coveted gold plates of the auction were Monsieur Aigle, Madame Cigogny, Marie-Julie, and Monsieur Cartier sitting at a table at the other end of the room. The other lucky ones were Oberon Bernard and Daniel Drago, located two tables away from them. Looking to his left, Henri also found signs for the right to participate in the auction from Monsieur Oak and Loup, four tables from him on one side of the room.

'Dear friends, I could not resist the temptation to become the host of the evening,' Mila began playfully, rising from her place of honor and going to the stage. 'Not in this stunning outfit, because hiding it at the banquet table would be just a crime,' she added in a manly way, having received the satisfied exclamations of the guests who appreciated the joke.

'You know, it is customary to start such events with minimal rates, but… I like to start a meal with dessert, especially if the first dish on the menu is fugu fish.' The guests laughed and after waiting for the necessary pause, she continued, 'Please, welcome lot number one! Starting price is two million four hundred thousand US dollars!'

The hall immediately exploded in whispers when the lot itself was taken to the center of the room on a small silver cart covered with a dark velvet blanket.

'So, before you is our first treasure,' she added at the moment when her assistant removed the cloth covering the lot and in front of the guests' eyes on a transparent plastic tray dotted with countless semi-precious stones, among which Henri examined several purple charoite stones, on this very tray stood…an ordinary glass of water?

'Isn't that too much for one?' Chuck Aigle asked in a serious tone.

Most of the room immediately exploded with laughter and applause, except for the auction participants, who, like Chuck, were extremely serious.

'I'm ready to take it upon myself,' said a slightly flustered Oberon.

'You?' Chuck chuckled. 'Thank you for being admitted to this auction at all. The Fund should have been renamed Septima a long time ago.'

'Formally, my candidacy is much more suitable than all those present here,' he objected.

'I can't help but agree that the Bernard family owns this issue,' Oak reasoned aloud.

'But that's almost three times more than you can afford,' Aigle went on, not taking his eyes off Oberon.

'I'll make him a loan,' Daniel Drago said calmly as he sipped his Banana Dynasty cocktail. 'Because I can,' he added, glancing pointedly at the taken aback Chuck.

'So, my congratulations, friends! Lot number one goes to Monsieur Oberon Bernard,' Mila announced to friendly applause. 'Well, without thinking twice, I propose to move on to the next lot of our auction.'

At the very moment when the next lot was brought into the center of the hall, Henri's heart froze so that its knocking did not interfere with the pleasure of contemplating the beauty that appeared before him.

'Before you is a majestic 1200-year-old ficus bonsai. It is more than two centuries older than its famous brother from the Italian Crespi.' The tree that occupied the central part of the hall seemed to consist of a thousand small branches twisted around each other and united into three large trunks. The bonsai was almost three meters high, which made its peaks almost inaccessible.

'And what is the price of this issue?' asked Monsieur Oak indifferently, neatly adjusting massive glasses in a thick wooden frame.

'All this splendor is yours for only three and a half million US dollars,' Mila added smiling, walking up to the tree.

'I intend to compete with you, Monsieur Oak, and raise the bid to four million.' Madame Cigogne joined in the bidding evenly and confidently.

'Well,' Oak replied with a leisurely sigh, 'I am ready to give it to you Madame Cigogne. I am sure that you will take care of the tree in the best possible way, and if you have any problems or questions, I am always happy to help you,' he finished, nodding politely to her at the opposite end of the room.

'Thank you, Monsieur Oak; it's a pleasure to deal with you, as always.' Cigogne nodded in response.

'Ladies and gentlemen, lot number two goes to Madame Cigogne. Our congratulations!' Mila announced, applauding.

'What an unusual auction today,' whispered Henri's neighbor sitting on the right, who seemed to be one of the shareholders of the Trust.

'I can't disagree,' Henri replied, trying to feign surprise.

'Our next lot will be highly appreciated by lovers of ancient culture and the art of hunting.' Mila made a dramatic pause, giving the staff time to bring an exhibit covered with a silver blanket to the center of the hall. Before you is the original of the bronze sculpture "Artemis with a deer," dating back to the first century BC. The starting price is three and a half million US dollars.

'Gentlemen, here I am decisively entering the game,' raising the gold plate with her right hand, Marie-Julie, who was sitting at the table opposite Henri, finally spoke up. Come to think of it, this was the first time in nineteen years that he had seen her face that close. Right now, he saw in front of him the same huge eyes, a narrow nose, dark skin, and even freckles. Still the same Marie-Julie as nineteen years ago, but something elusive about her had changed a lot over the years. After reflecting on the reason for the changes, Henri concluded that it was most likely in the unusual expressions on this face. Expressions that this person had never exactly assumed before in his presence.

'A goddess will certainly get along better with another goddess,' Chuck Aigle began flatteringly, provoking general approval, 'but as far as I know, this amount is high enough for you. But I, on the contrary, just have this amount, so I would like to compete with you.'

'Wouldn't like,' Marie-Julie corrected him, placing her right hand on his shoulder. 'It's customary to say "I wouldn't like to compete with you,"' she said, smiling. 'I accept your generous offer to lend the required amount of funds and appreciate our friendship.'

'Yes…' Chuck agreed reluctantly, squeezing out a smile, literally drop by drop. I'm always glad to help you, Mademoiselle Langlaist.'

Lot number three goes to Mademoiselle Marie-Julie Langlaist. Our congratulations! announced Mila nodding approvingly toward the winner.

Henri did not take his eyes off Marie-Julie for about a minute until she straightened a strand of hair with her right hand.

'Right hand again,' he said inwardly, continuing to follow her. 'For the eighth time in the evening, she unconsciously prefers to use her right hand, which is very suspicious considering that she is left-handed. She was left-handed anyway.'

'Well... Our auction is gaining momentum steadily approaching the equator. Before announcing the next lot, I want to raise this glass to the co-founders of tonight, my closest friends and part-time members of the board of directors of the East End Investment Company: Yahon Moble, Gerld Electric, Ivy Cecilia Bella Cedric, Cyrus Cecil Black, and John Paul Morgan Chatwin... Without you, tonight would not have been possible because just a year ago the very idea of a merger between the East End Investment Company and the Octava Trust Fund seemed almost impossible to me. Oh, and, of course, some words in honor of my future husband, Monsieur Jules Emmanuel Lero, who, perhaps later, will nevertheless agree to change his last name to Crule.' The audience burst into deafening applause. 'He has not yet formally agreed to change his surname, but no one can refuse me. Only not in this outfit.' Pityingly knitting her eyebrows in a house, she went up to him and stretching out her hand, received such a hotly begged kiss. 'Well, he agrees,' she concluded to a general ovation.

'Olya-la, what a busy evening we have.' Again going to the center of the hall, Mila continued, 'I will not hesitate and hasten to address all connoisseurs of popular art gathered here today. We ask you to welcome the original work of the incomparable Andy Warhol – the audience burst into applause once again when the legendary silver canvas, depicting eight overlapping iconic images of Elvis Presley from the movie "The Flaming Star" was brought into the center of the room. So, before you, the world-famous "Eight Elvis." The starting price of this masterpiece is three million US dollars.'

'Before all of you start to...' Chuck began, expecting to be interrupted, but seeing that no one had raised a sign except him, he asked uncertainly, 'What, just like that, without a fight at all?' slyly smiling with the corners of his mouth, he clarified.

'It's unlikely that you'll find anyone equal here,' Oberon began, rubbing his palms. 'Pop art is yours. I remember how he brought eighteen disks of some fashionable punk bands to our boarding school, and just two weeks later, everyone around began to listen to it. Even I, an insane fan of Stravinsky and Tchaikovsky, also got hooked on it.' The audience was filled with general laughter.

'Well, as they say, flawless victory. Lot number four was won by Monsieur Chuck Aigle.'

To general applause, the painting left the hall, after which another silver cart covered with blue velvet took its place.

'I confess that the next lot is perhaps one of the most attractive for me. What is there to hide? As the hostess of the evening, I wanted to appropriate it. Well, as a wedding present,' Mila said sarcastically, blinking innocently, again making most of the hall smile. 'But, as you know, we are already one big family with the members of the fund, and it is customary to share with the family. So, I present to you my treasure. Before you are the incomparable statue of Venus of Willendorf, dating back to 25,000 BC.'

The assistant standing next to the cart with a light movement threw off the blanket from the lot, allowing the audience to personally contemplate a figurine made by people of the late Paleolithic period, whose outlines strongly resembled the silhouette of a naked pregnant woman.

'The starting price is four million US dollars,' Mila added after a short pause.

The participants in the auction were looking at each other tensely, holding gold plaques at the ready. The naked eye could see how much they were worried about the fate of this lot and the fact that there would be a lot of applicants for it.

'I'll take it for four million,' Daniel Drago announced loudly as he stepped into the game.

'Raise the rate to four and a half million,' Monsieur Oak announced his intentions, as he sat spellbound, looking at the statuette.

'Five and a half million – and I stop trading,' Chuck said ultimately, putting his hand on top of a glass of bourbon.

'Seven million five hundred thousand dollars,' Daniel Drago said coldly, not even looking at his opponent. 'And I can raise the amount all night.'

'You don't have that sort of money,' Chuck replied with a dismissive breath and a grimace.

'Rather, this is your old information about MY MONEY,' Daniel replied, continuing to ignore his interlocutor with even a glance.

'I suppose this is the last word?' smiling, Mila clarified, looking from Monsieur Aigle to Monsieur Drago. Chuck thought about something in his mind for a second and hesitated a little, nevertheless nodded to Mademoiselle Crule. 'Seven million five hundred thousand dollars once, seven million five hundred thousand dollars two, seven million five hundred thousand dollars three. Sold! Congratulations to Monsieur Daniel Drago on your invaluable purchase!' The hall was filled with applause and a roar of discussion at such an expensive purchase.

'Wow! An incredible evening! Pack the Earth guys!' Mila turned over her shoulder to the assistants. 'They'll buy the whole planet, but in installments.'

The evening continued to gain momentum when one of the assistants came out to the center of the hall, holding in his hands a small silver tray on which a small…photograph rested peacefully?

'The time for our next lot has finally come. Dear friends, let me present to your attention the original of this iconic photograph, with an autograph left for the host of a famous program on the American CBS television channel, personally signed by one of the founders of modern theoretical physics and the luminary of the world science, Monsieur Albert Einstein.'

The guests applauded in chorus when they saw one of the originals of the iconic photograph of the scientist who stuck out his tongue, laughing in this way at all of humanity. Henri turned his attention to the participants in the auction and immediately caught a strong tension in their looks; it seemed that a lot of them had been waiting for this lot.

'The starting price for this lot is four and a half million dollars. Well, your bids, monsieur and madam,' Mila called, clearly anticipating a tumultuous auction.

'Four and a half million,' Monsieur Oak began without unnecessary drama.

'Raise to five million,' also without ceremony, continued Daniel Drago.

'Five, five hundred,' Chuck Aigle, who entered the auction, said, slightly loosening his tie, looking attentively at Monsieur Oak, sitting at the opposite end of the hall. Henri knew what that look meant. Most likely, Monsieur Oak's possibilities had been exhausted at this level and he was not able to take further part in the auction.

'Six million,' Ou announced calmly, shifting his gaze to the astonished Chuck Aigle, to whom at that moment the obscenely satisfied Monsieur Loup was waving.

'They cooperated...' Chuck grumbled in a whisper, sipping a sip of bourbon. 'Eight million,' he added loudly.

'It seems that we are brewing a small record here,' joyfully clapping her hands, Mila commented on the auction.

'Monsieur Aigle' – Monsieur Drago turned to face him for the first time in the auction – 'I propose a joint purchase.'

Theatrically raised eyebrows, Chuck silently tried to portray the highest degree of surprise, but after a few seconds, he answered, 'And I suggest checking how old my information is regarding your money. Mademoiselle Crule, I'm raising the rate to eight and a half million.'

'Fifteen million. Joint purchase of families Oak, Loup, and Drago.' Monsieur Oak indifferently held out, looking Chuck in the eyes.

Mr. Aigle at the same second turned his eyes to the maliciously smiling Daniel Drago, raising a glass in his honor.

'Fifteen million times... Fifteen million two... Fifteen million three! Sold! Oak, Loup, and Drago, congratulations!' The assembled cheers supported the holders of the shrine of the scientific world.

'Thank you all for your attention, it was truly a very exciting auction,' Mila said enthusiastically.

'What about the last lot?' Monsieur Aigle interrupted her, raising his eyebrows.

'Oh, you mean the golden bowl with the image of the two-faced god Janus?' Mila asked coquettishly. 'It's not a secret to anyone that I left her for myself as the hostess of the evening and the bride. I must have at least some dowry.'

'Oh, Mila! I would never deprive such a beautiful bride of her dowry,' Chuck continued his question with a smile. 'I'm talking about...'

'Gold disc,' Jules finished for him in a serious tone.

'It's not about Michael Jackson's Thriller, is it?' in bewilderment, one of the neighbors at his table asked Henri.

'The prototype of Voyager's gold disc,' Jules continued, looking at Needle. 'It belongs to the head of the Trust fund and I am now performing the powers of the head of the Trust by inheritance rights.' Jules snapped coldly, looking in turn at all the participants in the auction.

'But, this is a very... An overwhelming burden...' began Chuck, but he was immediately interrupted by Mila.

'It was a great auction, but like the uncontrolled internet, it quickly came to an end.'

'I think we should reconsider…' Monsieur Aigle entered, but at the same moment, he suddenly fell silent and froze with a picture of bewilderment on his face, and suddenly began to cough very loudly. In just a few moments, the cough quickly turned into an asthmatic attack, which caused him, like a fish thrown out on land, greedily swallowing air with his lips in an attempt to fill his lungs with it.

'Excuse me, did you say something?' spoke Tamil, coming closer to him. 'You can't be heard very well through this cough.' As bowing over him, she discreetly reached out to him a handkerchief, whispering, 'No more sounds.' Chuck extended his hand to the headscarf and, in panic, agreeing, nodded.

'The evening turned out to be so intense that some people get nervous,' she chirped, turning to the audience with a "madam charm" smile and having received cheers of approval, she immediately returned to her place, giving up the microphone to the host.

'Dear guests, it is almost midnight, which means that our gala evening is approaching its climax. Exactly eight minutes later, we will officially move on to the wedding ceremony between Mrs. Mila Nicole Crule and Monsieur Jules Emmanuel Leroy and after that, we will end the evening with the solemn inauguration of Monsieur Leroy as the chief custodian of the Trust.' The hall once again exploded with applause and Mila, arm in arm with Jules, went to the side scenes.

The organizers of the evening invited the guests to move from the banquet area to the center of the hall for a solemn buffet. After just two minutes, the tables were empty and everyone who came with glasses of champagne in their hands was impatiently awaiting the culmination of tonight. The closest to the stage, of course, were the honored guests of the ceremony, namely the director of the East End Investment Company and the heads of the founding families of the Octava Trust Fund.

Henri at this time absentmindedly looked at the glass dome above his head, still shaking from the heavy downpour. Reluctantly looking at his watch, he found the time was six minutes to midnight. Looking at the stage, he saw the deputy mayor delivering a solemn speech of the conjugal vow. Grabbing another Fall of Zion glass from the cocktail table, Henri stopped a little further from the main crowd. Four minutes to midnight.

'What a fortunate coincidence for Mademoiselle Crule. The merger agreement has already been signed and if the curse at the inauguration today overtakes Monsieur Leroy, Mademoiselle Crule, as his wife, will be able to take the post of Head Regent of the Octave.' Turning his head, Henri saw Monsieur Loup standing on the right.

'I thought you and the others took a seat in the front row,' Henri said without taking his eyes off the prize.

'As an old farsighted person, I can see everything more clearly from afar,' Loup said, sipping from a glass of champagne.

Jules and Mila were already signing the marriage certificate when Henri turned his gaze back to his watch. Three minutes to midnight.

'Dear guests, let me officially introduce you to Monsieur and Mademoiselle Crule,' the presenter announced loudly, causing a deafening wave of applause.

'Well, I told you. Nothing will ever change. The strong devour the weak,' Monsieur Loup whispered after draining his glass.

'Dear guests, now we are moving on to the final part of tonight. We are waiting for the inauguration of the new head of the Octave Trust Fund, Monsieur J…' the presenter began, but his speech was interrupted by the assistant to the Deputy Mayor who approached him.

'Dear friends, give us one minute, please.' The presenter quickly approached the newly made spouses and asked perplexedly, 'Monsieur and Mademoiselle Crule, the fact is that the assistant to the deputy mayor has just turned to me and… He claims that this marriage cannot be called valid.'

'What's the matter? We've checked everything with the lawyers a damn lot of times,' Mila shouted angrily, completely forgetting about decency. 'What more do you want?'

'The point is…' the deputy mayor, who approached them, began carefully, going through the papers, 'we have just received a message from the mayor's office and the fact is that this marriage cannot be called valid, since the archives indicate that Monsieur Leroy is already married. The marriage was contracted two days ago outside the country in Las Vegas and legalized this afternoon in Paris.'

The presenter who was standing nearby was so shocked by everything that was happening that in panic he forgot to turn off the microphone, which is why the last words of the assistant mayor about the preliminary marriage of Monsieur Leroy echoed through the hall, immediately causing a loud rumble.

'Well, how do you like this somersault, Monsieur Loup? Is life still able to surprise you?' Henri asked smiling, looking at his confused face.

The rumble in the hall did not subside and the furious Mila, pushing the presenter, walked abruptly toward the edge of the stage, addressing the VIP guests in the first row, 'Why the hell, didn't you check his marital status? You bunch of mindless idiots! Do I have to do everything myself?'

'Mademoiselle Crule, we only checked the last status this morning, most likely the legalization was completed just before the ceremony began,' one of its directors babbled in a trembling voice.

'What are you…' she said angrily as if throwing lightning with her eyes in their direction. 'Useless, empty, like…' Before the last word left her lips, all five immediately fell to the ground suffering in wild convulsions and blowing white foam from their mouths. The hall was seized by severe panic and screams of horror.

'Silence!' Raising her eyebrows, Mila turned to the audience, but there was no reaction to her words. 'I told everyone to be silent…' she whispered, and to Henri's surprise, all two hundred people at that very second just…froze!

'Am I still alive?' Henri frantically asked his brain, seeing two hundred people in front of him motionless, like chess pieces. 'You seem to be alive,' the brain immediately told him, ordering his eyes to blink. Slowly shifting his gaze to his hands, he gently moved first with his left hand, then with his right. Putting his glass on the floor, he walked slowly toward the stage, through hundreds of frozen figures that resembled statues. The fact that among the chipped guests would be the heads of the families – the founders of the foundation, Henri more than expected, but the fact that all those gathered in the hall, including the staff, were among them, caused him a genuine shock.

Standing in front of one of the guests, Henri carefully felt his pulse. So far, everything was normal. Exhaling with relief, he cautiously walked through the forest of living statues to the stage where Mila continued to torture her directors while talking with the heads of families – the founders of the foundation, who, by her grace, also remained conscious.

'I don't want to be harsh with you,' she said sympathetically, shaking her head. 'But you leave me no choice.'

'My darling, you were so busy all this evening that I didn't have time to tell you how incredibly good you are in white,' Henri said enthusiastically, stopping by the stage.

'Henri, my soul. Maybe at least you will explain to me what is happening here?' she said nervously, watching him waving to Jules standing behind her on the stage.

'There was a passion. Crazy and unbridled passion. I confess that I introduced them. Although initially, Mademoiselle Crane was madly in love with me,' Henri explained actively gesticulating.

'Crane?' Mila cried out in disbelief, knitting her eyebrows in shock.

'Thomas somehow managed to create a controller?' said Marie-Julie, smiling at Jules, cautiously. 'Otherwise, you would never have dared to take such a daring step.'

'Controller?' Oberon wondered looking from Marie-Julie to Henri.

'Yes, like the one Mila is now running the entire hall with,' Marie-Julie explained, adding, 'how did you manage to bypass Thomas's blockage?'

'The blocking was temporary, it was laid down in the program he wrote,' Henri answered cautiously, not wanting to disclose the details of the operation carried out in America.

'It was necessary to get rid of him three years ago, as I suggested,' said Monsieur Oak, continuing to calmly sip champagne.

'Three years ago we were too busy trying to get rid of Drago once again,' Madame Cigogne said indifferently.

'What?' Drago cried in bewilderment.

'No, that was four years ago. And three years ago we once again played off the Aigle family with the Bernards,' corrected Monsieur Loup, who appeared out of nowhere.

'You don't need to look at us so condemningly, Henri,' continued Marie-Julie, smiling and not taking her eyes off him. 'It was your grandfather who started this high-tech race.'

'Yes, my grandfather acted monstrously, but he wanted to end the endless string of deaths that had been spreading behind the Trust fund since its inception,' Jules replied, knitting his eyebrows.

'Finish? Of course, not having any involvement in the long string of miscarriages in the Kebe family that occurred every time a male Guardian could appear in the Trust,' Mila said, laughing. 'Apparently, the lives of the men of the Kebe family are not as important as the lives of the men of the Lero family.'

'Interesting… Was compassion included in the list of conditions for the takeover of hundreds of thousands of companies that you bankrupted? Lands that you have caused environmental disasters? And the hundreds of "accidental" murders that accompany all these cases?' began Henri with a challenge looking into her eyes. 'We do not make excuses for grandfather. He was as much a monster as the rest of you. You cannot kill for good. Death is death.'

'Monsters?' she asked hysterically, throwing up her hands. 'The first time the members of the foundation visited our home, I was eleven. I remember this evening well. Outside, it was raining heavily and the thunderstorm did not subside for the third day in a row. Mother, as usual, played bridge with the servants and my brother tortured the violin. A dull, unremarkable evening, if not for a few strangers who burst into our house. They were wet, frightened, gloomy, and in such a hurry that they did not even close the front door behind them. Standing at the doorstep, they begged their father to take some samples with him as soon as possible and quickly go with them to the clinic. Having run out onto the veranda for my father, I saw a parking lot in front of the house, in which, shuddering with tears, Monsieur Langlais was sitting in the back seat, clutching a very young curly-haired girl covered in blood in his hands.' Mila carefully moved to the middle of the stage. 'Marie-Julie was the first to have the chip installed after her death.'

Henri looked cautiously at the smiling Marie-Julie. It means that that evening he really saw her there… And instead of help, he simply flew, convincing himself that all this was just a figment of his imagination. Having removed the responsibility from the soul, he simply closed his eyes.

'The chip was digitized for my brother Charles, so it doesn't always work as we would like,' Marie-Julie commented quietly. 'Charles was an idealist and so resisted the idea of external control so I had no choice. My father was against my candidacy, and Charles was against it so much that he could simply shoot himself in such a way as to deliberately damage the brain.'

'Where is he now?' asked Henri slowly digesting what he heard.

'In the same place as your brother Thomas. I did not stop the tragedy, but only postponed it. The only difference is that the cause of his death was not the chip itself, but me. He hanged himself the same evening when I visited him in the Seoul hospital for the first time in seven years… Charles kept shouting that it was unnatural. That it was no longer me, but a living corpse, mocking the body of his poor sister… We did not start this war, Henri. Whatever one may say, but the Lero couple deserved what they received, during those years of clowning, in which they fooled all of us, portraying the dead. Although… Thomas was not like that.'

'Thomas, like Charles, was an idealist, but unlike Charles, he was an active idealist,' Mila said irritably. 'During these nineteen years, he was able to give us a lot of trouble. Sharp and nauseatingly correct. Strong, but so weak in this correctness, like all the righteous.'

'Weak like that?' Taking the controller out of the inner pocket of his jacket, Jules raised his eyebrows inquiringly.

'Hmm… So you didn't install it into the chip after all?' coming closer, she whispered in bewilderment. 'Then…did you get him out? As the assistant mayor said, the marriage seems to have taken place in Las Vegas? It's not that far from Los Angeles. How is Dr. Laocoon doing?'

'He asked to apologize for not being able to come to the celebration,' Henri replied as coldly as possible.

'So you had time to see your father and uncle?' folding her arms over her chest, Mila asked cautiously.

'Was that you?' Jules addressed Mila in a trembling voice.

'Is the executioner the one who kills, makes a decision, or passes a sentence? Or everyone who votes for this decision, or in general everyone who takes part in the vote?' looking in his direction, she asked. 'They revealed themselves. Had they not entered the game again, we most likely would not have found them. There is no malice here, we are not a bunch of sociopaths. Just business – and nothing more.'

'Well then,' said Jules, raising his thumb over one of the buttons of the controller. 'You will understand me. Nothing personal.'

'Now that's interesting,' she continued playfully, folding her arms across her chest. 'I suppose you know that I have the same thing in my head. So your toy won't kill me for sure. I'm afraid she won't even cripple me.'

'Do not equate us with yourself. It shouldn't kill or injure anyone,' Henri answered disdainfully, putting his hands in his trouser pockets.

'So Thomas managed to add the blocking function to the controller?' Straightening his glasses, Monsieur Oak was amazed.

'It was Henri. He's a specialist in neuroprostheses,' Jules answered proudly, nodding toward his brother.

'Thank you,' Henri commented, looking down at his feet.

'You're generally a very smart guy when you're not distracted by skirts,' Oberon said sarcastically.

'I?' Henri cried in amazement, turning his head toward Oberon.

'Ever since the boarding school,' Chuck Aigle confirmed, nodding approvingly at Marie-Julie.

'To this day,' Mila agreed.

'Yes, it's time to tie it up,' Jules stated, turning to his brother.

Now? Do we want to discuss this now? Seriously? raising his left eyebrow, Henri wondered.

'It pushes me to be frank in especially critical situations,' Chuck said, not taking his eyes off Henri. 'By the way, it's time for you to get your hair cut.'

'Is everyone here aware that the fate of humanity is at stake?' Unable to withstand an awkward pause, the silent Cartier suddenly entered the conversation. 'Just in case, I want to clarify.'

'I fully support that,' Henri continued, nodding toward Cartier. 'Strictly speaking, by locking, we mean rather full formatting. All data regarding the chip will be permanently deleted, plus two to seven years before installation. Depends on individual characteristics,' Henri said, looking around at the others.

'Now it becomes clear why Thomas made the deal,' Mila said, biting her lip.

'A deal?' Henri looked from Mila to Jules in confusion.

'Almost immediately after the installation of Jules's chip, your father decided to initiate Thomas into the affairs of the Trust. Then he, most likely, decided not to follow the path trodden by your grandfather and, having worked on a neurochip, created his system on its basis with protection so perfect that he issued an ultimatum to your father to resign. That year, your father feigned his death and moved to the United States to live with your uncle. Thomas managed to build an ideal defense against outside interference not only for himself and Jules but also for all the microchipped members of the Kebe family. With this system, although it was perfect, we still found one small gap,' Mila said with a smile, looking at the eldest of the brothers Lero.

'I didn't have an aneurysm or other surgical interventions that could disguise the installation,' Henri objected, catching the train of her thoughts.

'Oh, are you so sure of that?' asked Mademoiselle Crule, pacing the stage with her hands folded behind her back. 'Hmm... Where do you start? It seems that it was a rainy evening when the car with the still young Jules and Henri flew off the track. Remind me how many hours after the accident did you wait for your aunt's friends at that gas station?'

Henri silently froze in horror, clutching the figurine Thomas had left for him in his jacket pocket.

'You don't remember, do you? You just passed out, right there, in pain, and woke up in the hospital. Young Henri was too proud to mention the broken arm in conversation with his aunt and too proud to ask anyone else for help. Workers found you at a telephone booth opposite a gas station, already bleeding out. You didn't just have a chip implanted that night, Henri, you got it installed after you died. In this, you were the second after Marie-Julie, and just like in her case, your chip was digitized for your brother. Hence, your trembling in your left hand with great excitement. Thomas was left-handed, right?'

Henri looked confusedly from Mila to Marie-Julie and then to Oberon.

'Nothing personal, Henri. Of course, you are very nice to me, but I love money more,' Oberon defended himself guiltily, spreading his hands.

'Your family is somewhere in Australia, I suppose,' Henri suggested, realizing that the whole story with the fire was just a play.

'Nearby. You correctly guessed the hemisphere,' he confirmed, finishing his glass of champagne.

'You sent people to the Seoul hospital for rehabilitation after installing the chips, right?' asked Henri, rubbing his palms.

'And you worked productively for one day in a mental hospital. And what have we not foreseen?' Mila asked with a puzzled frown.

'A patient who escaped with us,' Henri said slowly.

'Your informant?' Oberon began rounding his eyebrows. 'Although the fact that she turned out to be a patient explains a lot in her behavior.'

'Anyway, your chip is quite old and it is impossible to modify it, so you were our main lever of pressure on Thomas,' Mila said, correcting her hair. 'I then naively believed that it was just blind brotherly love, but... This guy was so smart that he not only blindly saved your life, but, having reached a dead-end in research and having almost no one around whom he could Trust, did bet on you. He believed in you so much that he even gave his life just to convince your skeptic soul to go into this water and continue his work. Thomas programmed his chip to destroy exactly five minutes before the time supposed by the "curse," setting a precedent at the cost of his own life. But what is his life on the scale of the fate of mankind? *So, most likely,* he thought. And now you just take and cross out all his victims, putting yourself in jeopardy? You are the only one who owns information about the controller. You understand very well that we may be among the first, but not the only ones who own such technologies. If you format us, you will touch yourself. And then all future attempts to forcibly establish total control will not be stopped.'

Jules shifted his worried gaze to his brother.

'She's bluffing. The neurochip would have betrayed itself several times, if it were true. And why can I still move?' Henri said confidently answering the mute question of his brother.

'Thomas could make sure you get a locking device installed. For example, at your dentist's in Hong Kong,' Mila suggested with a shrug.

'Even if it is…' Henri began when he felt the barrel of a pistol on the back of his head.

'Double the stakes,' Mila continued playfully clapping her hands. 'Let Jules press the button and if I am wrong, then the remaining Henri, who does not have a chip in his head, will be shot in the head by my man. By the way, this is Monsieur Basil; you met with him on the day we met at a charity reception.'

Fine, Henri thought, *I'm going to be shot by the "perch" from the anti-corruption reception.*

'Just press the button, Jules. Don't listen to her.'

'I would think hard before doing that.' Mila warned, moving her head nervously. 'If, of course, your brother is dear to you.' Jules convulsively turned his eyes from Mila to Henri.

'Jules, Jules! Look at me… Remember Los Angeles. Do you think she trusts anyone? She even chipped the dogs, what can we say about her people,' he said, looking his brother in the eye, adding, 'trust me.'

'But…' Jules began.

'And if "but," then you can do everything,' Henri interrupted him with a smile.

No matter what happens next, he still spent the last thirteen days of his life with his younger brother. Even if these were very chaotic days. Besides, Henri was still able to let go of his guilt for the death of Marie-Julie, sort out his relationship with his father, finally see Jiwon, call Lu, apologize to Laocoon, become interested in a patient in a psychiatric hospital, who, by the way, became his brother's fictitious wife, and finally, make a posthumous reconciliation with Thomas, who had never been in any kind of enmity with him. Jules will not be left alone; all these people will help him cope with everything. Together they will overcome everything. Henri once again confidently nodded to his younger brother, after which, taking a deep breath, Jules pressed the cherished button.

One of Henri's frequent excuses every time he was asked by his aunt or colleagues why he hadn't had children at thirty-three was his favorite "lack of cravings due to the childhood trauma of his older brother with a large age difference from the rest of the children." People usually call this the eldest child-nanny. Henri perfectly remembered the very small, eternally serious Thomas, who constantly needed to read and then disassemble and assemble equipment with him and glue aircraft models. Even better, he remembered as a little boy the always smiling kid, Jules, who required frequent walks in the yard to track down the neighbor's cats, an artistic assessment of his children's drawings, and endless requests to give him a ride on his back.

In this longest second in Henri's life, when the button pressed by Jules slowly lowered onto the controller panel, he clearly remembered the first day of their acquaintance. That evening, everyone was madly bustling about, waiting for Mom from the hospital and only the grandfather, calm, as always, was drinking tea in the living room, at the same time swearing at the newspapers he was leafing through. Unexpectedly, everyone in the yard heard the beep of his father's Facel Vega, and a minute later a proud father, a smiling uncle, and a mother beaming with happiness with a baby in her arms entered the house. Henri was about to come closer to get a better look at the baby, but Thomas was ahead of him, rushing into the hallway from the kitchen in a whirlwind, bringing with him a large scarlet apple, which he had carefully plucked from a neighbor's apple tree.

The beaming Thomas slowly walked closer to Jules, but when he brought the apple to the baby's head, his face changed instantly. He seriously thought about something for a minute and finally realizing that the apple was about the same size as the head of the newborn, he was very upset, realizing that he could not treat him to them. The funniest thing in this story was not the embarrassed face of Thomas and not even the surprised faces of his uncle and parents, but the contradictory relaxed-tense expression on the face of little Jules. The same expression with which at that very split second he was now looking at Henri across the entire room.

A moment and…a rumble. From a sharp sound, Henri involuntarily closed his eyes and caught himself thinking that all this time he was again clutching the anime figure left for him by Thomas in his jacket pocket in his palm. Another moment and…a sharp slap on the left hand.

'Where we will go now?' Opening his eyes, he saw in front of him a smiling Jules, holding his left shoulder. Looking around, Henri saw all two hundred guests of the evening lying supine on the floor. Monsieur Sudak, who put a pistol to the back of his head, as you might guess, was also among them. Henri slowly raised his head to the glass dome above their heads. The downpour was finally over.

'On the roof. Let's take some more wine,' Henri blurted out, heading to the banquet table for clean glasses and a couple of bottles of the incomparable 1947 Chateau Cheval Blanc.

Climbing upstairs, the brothers sat comfortably next to the central dome enjoying the view and recalling the millions of stories that happened to them over the past nineteen years.

The time was approaching dawn when most of the guests of the celebration had already woken up and went home in complete bewilderment.

How much do you think they will forget? looking down at the departing guests, Jules thought.

'Ninety-five percent of those present in the hall are about four years. The Heads of the families – the founders of the Trust and Tamil with the directors of the East End company – are on average about ten years and Marie-Julie…' Henri hesitated a little. 'She will start all over again. Only memories will go away, but her knowledge, skills, and experience will remain with her,' he continued, sipping his glass.

'Her chip was digitized from Charles and yours from Thomas since our father understood that you would be moving away from your mother's death for a very long time. Does this mean that…' Jules was quiet looking around at the pre-dawn city as if looking around for the right word.

I don't know. It's hard to say... How much is Charles in her chip and Thomas in mine? Have we learned something from them, and who are we now? the elder brother thought, reclining on his back.

'By the way, what are we going to do with the Trust?' asked Jules, as he admired the first rays of dawn.

'Hmm... I suggest reorganization. Did you get your hands on the Gold Disc?' Henri asked in a whisper, rising sharply and patting his brother on the shoulder.

'Are you serious?' Dumbfounded looking at his brother, the younger was perplexed. 'Shall we deal with satellites?'

'No,' Henri answered skeptically. 'Who needs a satellite when we can create a space ark?'

'And what do we call it?' asked Jules with a smile looking at the rising sun.

'"The Torch?"' whispered Henri, admiring the sunrise, taking out of his jacket pocket the figure that had accompanied him all these days, left for him by Thomas.

'"The Torch!"'

The End

CPSIA information can be obtained
at www.ICGtesting.com
Printed in the USA
BVHW052308290123
657301BV00003B/179